THE FOURTH GRADE WIZARDS

Barthe DeClements says, "When I was working as a school psychologist in Seattle, I was reevaluating a student whose file indicated that she had done adequate work in the elementary grades and then suddenly deteriorated. Now, after several years, it was obvious from her performance on my tests that she was again functioning at an average level.

"I asked the girl what had happened the year she began her decline. 'Oh,' she said, 'that was the year my mother died.'

"'And what has happened to you this year?'

"'My dad got married again.'

"'What do you call your new stepmother?' I wanted to know.

"'I call her Mom.'

"'And what does she call you?'

"It was from the memory of this girl's answer that I drew the ending of Marianne's story."

"DeClements incisively reports on grade-school life . . . Entertaining."

—*Kirkus Reviews*

PUFFIN BOOKS BY BARTHE DECLEMENTS

The Fourth Grade Wizards

BY BARTHE DeCLEMENTS

Puffin Books

*This book is dedicated to my two delightful
grandsons, Scott and Kevin. And to their
lovely mother, Nicole.*

PUFFIN BOOKS
A Division of Penguin Books USA Inc.
375 Hudson Street, New York, New York 10014

Penguin Books Ltd, 27 Wrights Lane, London W8 5TZ, England
Penguin Books Australia Ltd, Ringwood, Victoria, Australia
Penguin Books Canada Ltd, 10 Alcorn Avenue, Toronto, Ontario, Canada M4V 3B2
Penguin Books (N.Z.) Ltd, 182–190 Wairau Road, Auckland 10, New Zealand

Penguin Books Ltd, Registered Offices: Harmondsworth, Middlesex, England

First published in the United States of America by Viking Penguin,
a division of Penguin Books USA Inc., 1988
Published in Puffin Books, 1990
10
Copyright © Barthe DeClements, 1988
All rights reserved

LIBRARY OF CONGRESS CATALOGING IN PUBLICATION DATA
DeClements, Barthe.   The fourth grade wizards/by Barthe DeClements.   p.   cm.
Summary: After her mother dies, Marianne becomes a daydreamer
and begins to fall behind in her schoolwork.
ISBN 0-14-032760-6
[1. Death—Fiction.   2. Remarriage—Fiction.   3. Schools—Fiction.]   I. Title.
[PZ7.D3584Fo 1990]   [Fic]—dc20   89-36026

Printed in the United States of America

Contents

ACKNOWLEDGMENT

I would like to thank the staff and students of Frank Wagner Intermediate School in Monroe, Washington, for sharing their school experiences with me. I am especially grateful to Dr. Jim Lattyak, Diane Shalander and her fourth grade class, and Carolyn Davisson and her fifth grade class. It was Jim Lattyak and his staff who originated the Master Wizard concept.

Christopher Greimes, Mari Greimes, and Nicole Southard gave me invaluable help with the manuscript in progress. And my editor, Deborah Brodie, with her wonderful sense of humor and endless patience, deserved, at last, a gentle story.

B.D.

The Fourth Grade Wizards

Your Name's on the Board

Every student in our fourth grade class was supposed to be sitting up straight. Our eyes were to be on the blackboard where Miss Jewell was dividing rectangles into little boxes. "Now," she said, "this rectangle has three equal parts. If I shade this part, what part of the rectangle is shaded?"

As Miss Jewell scribbled in one of the boxes with her chalk, my eyes turned toward the windows. The white house across the street reminded me of the house where I used to live. I put my head down on my desk and thought about my mom.

First, I imagined her in the living room of our old

house. Then I changed my mind and put her in the kitchen. She was bent over the oven door, checking the oatmeal-raisin cookies. When they were done, we ate them at the table which was covered with the blue flowered cloth.

I reached for my third cookie while Mom explained that she hadn't really died. People only thought she had. She really had been thrown from the airplane into some bushes. When the police went through the burned wreck of the jetliner, they didn't see her behind the bushes . . .

"Marianne!" Jack whispered. "Sit up."

Slowly I raised my head.

"Sit up straight." He had turned around in his seat. "Your name's on the board."

I looked at the left side of the blackboard. Below the word *Recess* were L.T. and S.H. Lindsey Todd and Sharon Hinkler had probably been talking. Below their initials was M.R. for Marianne Rawlins. My face burned with embarrassment. Jack turned back around, but it was too late.

"Someone else hasn't been paying attention." Miss Jewell leaned away from her rectangles and wrote J.H. below the M.R. My face burned hotter. Now I'd gotten Jack into trouble.

I paid strict attention while Miss Jewell asked for a

definition of a numerator and a denominator. Jack raised his hand. So did most of the other kids. I didn't.

Miss Jewell called on Diane who said a denominator meant how many equal parts something is cut into. A numerator meant how many parts we were talking about. That was a big help. I wanted to put my head down again, but I didn't dare.

When recess time came, Miss Jewell called on the rows with the good kids first. Sharon's row was next to last. Our row was last.

In front of me, Jack slunk down in his seat while the kids lined up. I whispered, "I'm sorry, Jack."

He shrugged and whispered back, "No big deal."

When all the kids had filed out of the room, Miss Jewell suggested that Sharon, Lindsey, and Jack study their spelling words. She had me come up to the blackboard. She drew a circle with her chalk, made a line through the middle, and whitened in the lower part.

"What part is shaded?" she asked me.

"Half," I said.

"How do I write a half?"

I thought a minute. "One on the top and two on the bottom."

"Good girl."

I nodded, relieved that she hadn't asked me which was the numerator.

"Would you mind staying in a little longer?"

I shook my head. "No."

"Jack, Lindsey, and Sharon," Miss Jewel said. "You can go out to recess now."

Jack zoomed out of the room. Sharon and Lindsey followed him to the door. I could see Jo Mae go down the hall. Sharon saw her, too.

"There goes that scummy Jo Mae," Sharon said to Lindsey.

Miss Jewell put down her chalk and marched across the room. "Sharon!" she said in a loud voice.

Sharon was halfway out the door, but she turned and came back in. A worried look was on her face.

Miss Jewell stared down at her. "Weren't you the girl who was in here crying last week because the boys called you a nark?"

"Yes, but . . . "

"And now I hear you calling another girl a name?"

"I know, but . . ."

"No buts!" Miss Jewell said firmly. "I don't like to be called names. You don't like to be called names. And I don't think Jo Mae likes to be called names either."

Sharon was wiggling all over trying to get her excuses in. "Yes, but Jo Mae is . . ."

"Yes, but Jo Mae has feelings just like you do. It's

time for you to begin treating everyone the way you'd like to be treated. Today!"

Sharon opened her mouth, looked at Miss Jewell's unsmiling face, closed her mouth, and went meekly out the door. As I watched her go down the hall, I gradually stopped shivering. I hate trouble.

Miss Jewell sighed, stopped by the coffee maker on the counter, and poured herself a cup of coffee. When she joined me at the blackboard, she put her free hand on my head. "Marianne, I know that sometimes you feel sad. I feel sad for you sometimes."

I knew she was talking about my mother. To keep from crying, I opened my eyes wide and sucked in my upper lip and bit it hard.

Miss Jewell's fingers combed through my long hair. "Even if you feel sad, the schoolwork has to be done. Right?"

I couldn't answer her.

"Right?"

"Right," I mumbled.

She gave me a bright smile and my head a little push. "Go on out to recess now."

The girls from my room were on the tetherball court. I got in line behind Diane. Sharon and Jenny were up. There's a long, white mark drawn on the cement to separate the players. Sharon kept stepping over the mark, which you're not supposed to do.

Diane poked me. "Come on, Marianne. You're third in line and that makes you the referee."

That was true. I watched Sharon and Jenny's feet closely. "Sharon, you're out," I called.

"What do you mean I'm out?" Sharon put her hands on her hips and glared at me. "I am not out." Jenny had stopped batting the ball and it swung slowly around the post, hitting Sharon in the back of the head. She whirled around. "Jenny, you did that on purpose."

"Well, you're supposed to . . ."

"Don't be a jerk, Sharon. You went over the mark about ten times." Diane shoved Tara forward. "Go on and play."

Instead of getting behind me to take another turn, Sharon stomped off the tetherball court. "I can't stand her," Diane said, as she watched her go.

Tara is the tallest girl in the room and she creamed Jenny and then she creamed Diane. When it was my turn up, I batted the ball as hard as I could so it swung over Tara's head. I stood way out and kept batting the ball hard until it wound around the top of the pole.

"Hey, way to go!" Diane yelled.

I held the ball still until Jenny took Tara's place. Jenny batted it once. I leaped high in the air, caught the ball a good one, and kept it going my way.

The bell rang before I got it wrapped around the pole. "You would have won, anyway," Jenny said. "I can't figure out how you do it. You're the smallest kid in the room."

We were almost to the school door. As Jack went past us, he tapped me on the shoulder. "You left your jacket out again."

I ran back to get my jacket, which I'd dropped on the ground before I was up. I'm always forgetting my jacket. About halfway home after school, I was glad I had one.

The sky had been clear in the morning. I thought I didn't even need a jacket, but my dad handed it to me at the door. "Take it," he told me. "It could be raining later."

And it was, too. Big drops. I ran down my street and up the steps to the apartment house, mumbling the rhyme my mom used to say: "April showers bring May flowers."

There weren't any spring flowers inside our apartment. Just brown walls and a fat, dark red chair and lumpy davenport. I went in the kitchen and took a carton of milk out of the musty-smelling refrigerator. No cookies. No brownies. That heavy, sick feeling was beginning to crawl over me.

I set my glass of milk on the coffee table in the living

room and sat on the lumpy davenport. I could turn on the TV. I didn't really want to watch TV. I slid down sideways and laid my head on my arms to start a daydream.

I tried to picture the white house. I tried to put my mom in the sunny dining room arranging yellow daffodils in her green vase. It didn't work. All I saw was the ugly, brown walls in front of me.

My mom wasn't ever going to come back. She was dead.

A Natural-Born Troublemaker

I was moping along to school the next morning when I saw Jo Mae. She was sitting on the sidewalk with her legs crossed and her head bent over the sole of a silver boot. She was going, "Oh, oh, ohhh."

I ran the half-block between us and crouched down beside her. "Are you hurt?"

She looked up at me, her face scrunched into lumps of misery. "No, I'm not hurt. It's this here ol' boot. I stepped on a rock and it went right through the worn part and made a hole."

She held her foot out for me to see. Sure enough, there was a hole with her yellow stocking peeking through it.

"I guess you'll have to get new shoes. Or get those fixed," I said. I thought it might be better if she wore running shoes, anyway. Those silver boots with their fancy decorations of colored stones were one of the things that Sharon Hinkler made fun of.

I stood up and dusted off my jeans. Jo Mae stayed on the ground, poking at the hole and moaning. "What am I going to do? What am I going to do? Now my sock will wear out."

"Well," I said, "walk over on the grass until we're on the school grounds. Then we can go in my room and get some cardboard from Miss Jewell. If you put that in your boot, it will last until you get home this afternoon."

She stood up, too, and brushed off the yellow skirt that matched her socks. The skirt was spotless, like everything else that Jo Mae wore. I could see, though, that it was mended in several places.

I walked quietly down the rest of the block with Jo Mae hopping beside me. I was thinking that maybe she wouldn't get another pair of shoes. Maybe she was poor and that was why she was also worrying about her stocking.

When we got into my classroom, Miss Jewell was there making coffee. I explained to her about the rock and the hole. She got out a piece of cardboard and helped us make a pattern for a new inside sole.

Jo Mae and I sat together at my desk while she cut out the pattern. "How does it fit?" I asked her when she tried the cardboard in her boot.

She stamped up and down. "Fine. I can't even feel it."

Miss Jewell was standing beside us, sipping her fresh coffee. "Um, Jo Mae, the PTA has a collection of used clothes. They keep them over at the administration building. I could take you there after school and we could see if they have some shoes in your size."

Jo Mae immediately became solemn. "Oh, no, ma'am. Our family don't take handouts."

Miss Jewell smiled down at her. "It isn't charity. When their children grow out of clothes, the mothers in the school district just gather them up for the PTA. The PTA keeps them for other children to use."

Jo Mae had turned her head to the side and was concentrating on the rules that were written on a poster hanging on the wall.

"Maybe the PTA would have some running shoes," I suggested to get her attention.

She kept looking at the poster. "I don't know if my daddy would like that."

"I tell you what," Miss Jewell said. "I'll give your mother a call and find out."

Jo Mae shot her one quick glance. "We live with my daddy's folks."

Miss Jewell nodded. "That's OK. I'm sure I can get the phone number from the office."

The first bell rang and Jo Mae turned to leave. "I thank y'all for your help."

When she said "help," it sounded more like "hep." After she was out the door, I asked Miss Jewell, "Is Jo Mae from the South?"

Miss Jewell laughed. "I think so."

The kids were piling into the room by then and I noticed something funny about Jack. At first I thought he had two lunch sacks. He put one on the shelf in the coat rack. The other one he kept sort of hidden by his side as he slithered up our aisle.

I was sitting in my seat when he went by me. "You swiped somebody's lunch," I said.

"No way." He had a wicked grin on his face as he took a wooden contraption out of the brown sack and carefully eased it into his desk.

I leaned clear over my desk to get a better look. "What's that?"

He slipped the thing forward a bit. "It's a spitball projector."

"You're kidding."

"No. See, you pull back this wire and put it into the

top of the clothespin. You put the spit wad against the rubber band that's hooked to the wire. And then you open the clothes pin and wham! Sharon gets it in the ear."

I slid down into my seat. "You're going to get in trouble."

"No. No way."

I pointed to the poster. " 'You will not throw anything in the classroom.' "

"I'm not breaking the rule. I'm not throwing anything. I'm just working my projector."

The second bell rang and Miss Jewell walked up to the front of the room to take roll. Jack leaned forward, hiding the opening to his desk. All I could see now was the back of his red head, but I knew he'd have a sweet, innocent look on his face.

We were doing reading when Jack first used his projector. I was back at the SRA kit, putting one orange card in and taking out another. I had just turned around to go to my seat when Sharon let out a yelp. I saw her put her hand on her neck and look wildly around the room.

Miss Jewell was bent over Tara's desk checking her scores. At the yelp, Miss Jewell glanced up at Sharon. "What's the problem?"

"Something just hit me." Sharon had her mouth drawn

into a tight knot as she glared first at Jack, who was busy reading and then at Lester, who held out his hands, showing he had nothing in them.

"Let's keep our attention on our work," Miss Jewell said and went back to checking Tara's answers.

I took my reading card to my seat. I had finished the story on it and was going over the second paragraph for the meaning of a word. As I was about to circle the answer "b," I saw Jack's shoulders hunch forward.

I moved to the side and stretched up so I could see into his desk. The spit wad projector was slowly being pulled out. One of Jack's hands disappeared toward his face and came back down to place a wet, gray blob of chewed paper on the rubber band.

The wire was slipped into the clothespin. The projector was pointed toward Sharon's head. I held my breath. Nothing moved.

I turned quickly to look for Miss Jewell. She was bent over Jenny's paper. I looked back at the projector. Jack's fingers were on the bottom of the clothespin. They squeezed. The rubber band zinged free and the gray blob flew through the air, landing on Sharon's pink barrette and dribbling into her hair.

I clamped my hand over my mouth to muffle my giggle as Sharon clamped her hand over the gray mess on her head. She took her fingers down and stared at them. "Oh, ick. Miss Jewell," she cried, "Miss Jewell!"

"OK," Miss Jewell said, standing up straight. "That will be all of that. Who is throwing the spit wads?"

Silence. I kept my eyes on Miss Jewell. I didn't dare look at Jack.

"Lester," she said, "have you thrown any spit wads today?"

"Me?" Lester pointed to his chest. "Not me. No way."

"Jack?" Miss Jewell was raising her eyebrows at him.

I scrinched down in my seat, afraid of what was to come.

"Do you mean did I *throw* a spit wad today?" Jack asked. "No, I did not *throw* a spit wad today."

Miss Jewell eyed him suspiciously.

Just at that moment, the door opened and Mr. Douglas, the principal, walked in. He's a huge man and my heart started to beat fast. But he didn't seem to pay attention to what was going on in the room. He just smiled at Miss Jewell and said, "The eagle flies."

She smiled back as she went over to him. He gave her an envelope from the pack he had in his hand. "Don't spend it all in one place," he told her.

She nodded happily. I guess principals think kids don't know that when the eagle flies it's paycheck time. You'd have to be real dense not to know, because the eagle flies at the end of every month.

Miss Jewell peeked inside her envelope before she put it in her purse. She seemed to have forgotten all about spit wads. When she got back to the front of the room, she told us to put our reading away and to take out our science books.

Sharon didn't forget about the spit wads, though. At recess she announced to us girls, "Just wait until I tell my mother that Miss Jewell didn't do anything about my getting hit in the head twice."

At the end of the day, I watched to see if Jack would take his projector home. He saw me watching him shake open his bag and stuff the contraption in. "Don't worry," he said. "I'll bring it back tomorrow."

The Unwanted Guest

I didn't see Jo Mae on the way home. Maybe she'd
gone with Miss Jewell, I thought. Maybe she'd get some
jeans and look like the other kids.

I slowed down as I came near the apartment house
where I lived. I hated the old brick building and its
smelly halls. When we'd moved in, my dad had said it
was only temporary. He said we'd get a new place soon,
but he never seemed to do anything about it. After
dinner, he mostly sat and stared at his newspaper.

Brittany was waiting for me at my door. She goes to
a religious school that gets out earlier than mine does.
I really didn't want to let Brittany in my apartment,

but I didn't want to hurt her feelings, either.

She followed me right into my bedroom. I tried to watch her while I hung my jacket in the closet. The hanger slipped off the pole, though, and I had to turn my head to put it on right.

Before I could get to her, Brittany had opened the jewelry box that was sitting on my dresser. "This looks so neat," she said, slipping on the garnet ring. "It just fits my finger."

I picked up the box and held it out. "Please put the ring back," I told her. "It's my mom's."

Brittany whirled away from me. "That doesn't matter. She's dead. Why don't you give me this for a present? Red matches me better than it does you. A blue stone would go better with your gray eyes. Is there a blue stone in there?"

I clapped the top shut on the box. "No, there isn't. And this jewelry is the only thing I have of my mom's. So please give me the ring back."

Brittany held her hand up to the light coming from the bedroom window. "Is this real? It looks pretty big to be real. Do you know if it is?"

"I think so. It used to be my grandmother's."

"Well, then, it wasn't your mother's in the first place. So you could give it to me. You've got more junk in there, anyway. You don't need it."

My stomach began to feel sick. I didn't know how to get the ring back from Brittany. I couldn't yank it off her finger. She's a fifth grader, and she's about twice as big as I am.

Brittany started for the door. "Let's go see if you have anything decent to eat."

I stayed where I was with my hand out. "Please give me the ring first, Brittany."

She turned on me. "Why do you need it?"

"Because it was my mom's."

"You've got a whole bunch of her junk. Don't be such a pig."

My breath was catching in my chest and I knew I was going to cry and I hated to. "Give it to me. Please give it to me." I reached up my arm to wipe my tears away.

Brittany's mouth curled down with disgust. She ripped the ring off and threw it at me. "Here, take it, baby!"

I crawled on the floor to get the ring from under the dresser while she laughed at me. "You're such a baby you can't even catch."

I put the ring in the box and put the box back on the dresser.

"Well," she said, "have you got anything to eat?"

"Just milk."

"Haven't you got anything decent like Oreos or popcorn?"

"No," I said quietly. "Maybe you should go back to your apartment if you're hungry."

"Oh, I'll drink the milk."

We sat together at the card table Dad had propped up in the kitchen. While Brittany drank her milk, she eyed my earrings. "You even get to wear earrings to school."

I touched one of the small gold loops in my ears. "My mother bought these for me."

"My mother spends all her money on the apartment or herself. She never buys me any pretty things." Brittany's mouth turned down and for a minute I thought she might cry. Instead, she plopped her glass hard on the table and the milk spilled over. I got up to get another napkin.

She seemed a little embarrassed as she watched me wipe up the spill. "This table sure is wobbly."

I threw the wet napkin in the garbage can under the sink before I sat back down. "I know. We're going to buy our own furniture when we get another house."

"What happened to your old house?"

"My dad didn't want to live in it after . . ."

"After your mother died? Did he think her ghost would come there or something?"

"No, I just think it made him feel bad." And me, too, I thought.

"You know what my mom says?" Brittany was leaning across the table and looking into my eyes. "My mom says it's about time your dad started to live a little. She's thinking of asking him over for a decent meal. Wouldn't it be neat if they got together since my mom's single and your dad's single? Maybe they'll buy a house together. They should get one with three bedrooms, though. Since you're younger than I am, we should have our own rooms. Don't you think so?"

I didn't answer that. The whole idea was so depressing I couldn't drink the rest of my milk. "I think I'd better do my homework now," I said.

After dinner, I curled up on the davenport beside my dad. "What do you do," I asked him, "when you can't get rid of someone you don't want in the house?"

He closed his newspaper and put his arm around me. "Did you have a fight with someone?"

"Well, kind of."

He thoughtfully pinched the bridge of his nose. "Hmm. If the person's a guest, I suppose you have to do the best you can with how they are. And make sure you're not doing anything to make it worse." He tilted his head at me. "That's not much help, huh."

"Not much," I agreed.

"I guess the important thing is to make sure you're

being nice. And then try to find something you both would like to play."

"Sometimes that's a little hard."

He was still thinking, I could tell. Before he could say any more, there was a knock at the door. I jumped up to answer it.

Mrs. James, Brittany's mother, was standing in the hall with a big smile on her face. Some of her bright, red lipstick was smeared on the bottom of her front teeth. "Is your daddy home, dear?" she asked me.

I said yes and opened the door wide for her to come in.

She went right up to my dad with her hand out-stretched. "I'm Josephine James. I think I've seen you in the laundry room."

Dad popped off the davenport and shook her hand. "Yes, yes, I think so. Won't you sit down?"

Mrs. James sat in the old chair. The broken springs let her sink down farther than she expected. She gave a little laugh and arranged her skirt before she told my dad, "Since Brittany and Marianne have become friends, I thought we should get to know each other."

My dad nodded and smiled and put the folded news-paper onto the coffee table.

"It's good they have each other to play with after school while you and I both work."

He nodded some more.

Mrs. James looked down, pressed her skirt over her knees, and then looked up at him through her long eyelashes. "Well, what I came to ask you is, would you and Marianne like to come to dinner next Saturday evening?"

That seemed to startle him. "Umm, I think we could. It would be a relief from my cooking."

I got up quick from my perch on the footstool so Dad couldn't see my face. I didn't want to spoil anything for him. "I think I'll get ready for bed," I said.

While I put my pajamas on, I could hear her high voice and his low voice as they said good-bye. I hopped into bed before the front door closed.

He came into my dark room. "You're not asleep already?"

"No."

"Do you mind going over there for dinner?"

"No, she's real pretty. And I guess you should live a little."

A laugh burst out from my dad. It was the first time I'd heard him laugh in months. He leaned down and kissed me good night. "It was Brittany you didn't get along with, huh?"

"Yes," I said.

"Well, we don't have to stay long after dinner. Just long enough to be polite."

I sure hoped so.

Jack Strikes Again

When I got to school the next day, I met Jo Mae in the hall. She was wearing jeans and running shoes, just like I'd hoped. "Hey, you're looking fine!" I told her.

She moved over close to me and whispered in my ear, "Don't tell anyone where I got the clothes."

I grabbed her by the neck and whispered back, "Don't worry, I won't."

There was a thump on my back. I turned around to see Jack behind me with his two lunch sacks. "Out of the way. Out of the way," he said. "You're blocking the halls."

I laughed and Jo Mae laughed as he marched on

into our room. "He must like you," she said.

Sharon stopped smack in front of us. "Who likes you?" she demanded.

I didn't say anything. Jo Mae didn't say anything. Sharon moved nearer the wall to get away from the pile of kids who were going to their classes. "Who likes you, Marianne?"

"Nobody. Jo Mae just thought someone in our room did."

"I bet it was Jack. He better not throw any spit wads at me today. If he does, my mother's going to talk to the principal." She eyed Jo Mae's new clothes. "I thought you only wore skirts to school."

"Not today." Jo Mae turned at the sound of the bell and went down the hall to her class.

Sharon watched her go. "That green T-shirt looks just like the one I had. It had a rip in the seam so my mother gave it to the PTA."

"I didn't see any rip in Jo Mae's shirt." I figured if there had been one, it would be mended now. Lucky for Jo Mae.

Miss Jewell started off our class with a bunch of stuff about the Heart Association contest. It was called a Jump-a-thon and we were supposed to get a permission slip signed by our parents and then get some sponsors for each minute we jumped and then jump rope at recess. I wasn't very interested because I'm not big on asking people for money.

When Miss Jewell said there'd be five kids on each team, Jack went into action. He made pointing motions at Lester. Lester nodded and pointed back. Tom pointed wildly at his chest and looked pleadingly at Jack. Jack nodded. Diane stared at Jack with her mouth dropped open. He nodded at her. Then he turned around to me and said, "You're on my team, too."

"I don't know any sponsors," I whispered.

"Don't worry. I'll get the sponsors." His voice sounded loud in the heavy silence. He whipped around in his seat. Miss Jewell was standing quietly with her eyebrows raised. "I'm sorry," Jack told her.

"Jack," she said with a big sigh, "you're never going to make Master Wizard."

You get to be a Master Wizard in our school if you're responsible, get all your work done, and have perfect behavior. My behavior was all right, but I didn't get my work done. Jack got all his work done, but his behavior needed improving. Diane was a Master Wizard until she mouthed off to the playground teacher and had to give her pin back.

Sharon's mother came to school to find out why Sharon wasn't given a pin. I don't know what the principal told Mrs. Hinkler, but Sharon still isn't a Master Wizard.

Jenny and Tara are. That means they can go in the hall, go to the bathroom, and go to the library without asking for a pass. They can leave the playground at recess and come into the building as long as they're wearing their pins.

All the stage crew and the office helpers are Master Wizards. You don't get to do much around the school unless you are one. All the kids want to be one, even though Sharon said her mother said it wasn't important. You get to hear a lot about Sharon's mother when Sharon's in your class.

After Miss Jewell passed out the Jump-a-thon permission slips for our parents to sign, we had reading. I started out doing the questions under "How Well Did You Read?" Pretty soon, though, I put my head down and began thinking about what it would be like if my mom lived in our apartment.

When I got home from school, Brittany would be waiting. Mom would open our door and tell Brittany she was sorry, but I couldn't play now. Then Mom and I would go inside and eat cake with German chocolate icing and Mom would tell me she had been in the hospital since she got rescued and she couldn't remember who she was, but when she got well, she remembered . . .

Miss Jewell tapped me on the shoulder. I sat up straight.

"Marianne," she said, "you simply have to pay attention to your reading. Most of the students are at least on the brown cards and you're way back on the orange cards. You're the only one in my class still on an orange card."

I looked down at my desk, totally ashamed.

She shook my shoulder a little. "Now, come on. Let's get to work."

I picked up the card and tried to focus on the third question. Miss Jewell went on to check Jack's scores. He was on a rose card, which is almost at the end of the reading kit.

Before she left him, Miss Jewell asked, "Jack, are you chewing gum?"

"No," he said, "I'm not."

Jack never lied. He wouldn't be chewing gum, I knew. He'd be chewing paper.

I finished "How Well Did You Read?" and was on "Learn About Words" when I noticed Jack's shoulders hunch forward. I looked around to see where Miss Jewell was. She was near the back wall, supposedly straightening books on the shelf. But she wasn't watching what her hands were doing. She was watching our corner of the room.

I didn't dare poke Jack. I faced the front and hissed at him. His hand went up to his mouth and down to

the side of his seat. I scrunched under my desk a little
and tried to kick him. My legs weren't long enough to
reach his.

I wanted to peek around to see if Miss Jewell was
still watching. I didn't dare do that, either. I hissed
again. Jack didn't seem to hear me.

I sat helplessly while Jack turned to the side and
squinted at Sharon, shifted his position back a little,
checked Sharon's head again, and shifted a little more.
Zingo! The gray blob landed on Sharon's chin.

She let out a yell. I heard Miss Jewell's high heels
hit hard on the floor as she marched toward Jack. Before I could swallow, she had him by the arm and out
of his seat. "You know the rules in this room."

"Yes, but I haven't broken any rules."

She turned him toward the poster on the wall. "Read
rule six."

" 'You will not throw anything in the classroom.' "

"Well?" she prompted him.

He looked up into her frowning face. "I didn't break
the rule. I didn't throw anything."

"That wasn't your spit wad that hit Sharon?" Miss
Jewell sounded so fierce I could hardly breathe.

"Yes, it was my spit wad, but I didn't throw it."

"Oh, then who did?"

"Nobody did."

Miss Jewell's eyes were glittering dangerously and I guess Jack thought he'd better tell her everything. He pointed to the contraption on his seat. "I really didn't throw it. The projector propelled the spit wad through the air."

Miss Jewell seemed confused. She dropped Jack's arm and stared at the contraption.

He picked it up, put it on his desk, and pulled at the thick rubber band. "See, you hitch this to the clothespin wire and put the spit wad in here."

The frown broke away from Miss Jewell's face. For a minute, I thought she was going to laugh. But instead, she took in a long breath and sucked in her cheeks. "I guess we'll have to make an addition to our rules."

She went up to her desk for her Magic Marker, went over to the poster, and wrote below rule six, "Or cause anything to fly through the air."

Sharon was watching all this with her chin stuck out and her lips pursed together. Miss Jewell turned and looked at her and then at Jack. "Jack," she said, "you may have technically circumvented the rule this time, but I think there are some other issues we need to deal with. You hurt Sharon . . ."

"Wet spit wads don't hurt," Jack said.

"Maybe they don't actually hurt, but I imagine they

sting. And it certainly bothers Sharon to be picked on. Why are you picking on her?"

We all looked first at Jack and then at Miss Jewell. Our whole class knew why he hated Sharon. She narked on him all the time. The last time she got him in trouble was when she told the playground teacher, Mrs. Wilson, that he'd said the F-word at recess.

Jack didn't answer Miss Jewell. He didn't tell on anybody. Not even Sharon.

"Well," Miss Jewell went on, "I think you need to make more than an apology to Sharon. I think you need to do something very nice for her. Nobody likes to be used for target practice. This is Friday. So by Monday morning I expect you to have thought up something nice that you can do to make Sharon feel better."

Sharon's chin relaxed. A pleased smirk spread over her face. Jack slunk down in his seat.

"Now let's get back to our reading," Miss Jewell said.

At recess, the boys all crowded around Jack, asking him what he was going to do for Sharon. He shoved his friends away and went up on the bars and hung down by his knees.

Sharon was watching all this from the tetherball court. When there was no more action around Jack, she turned her attention to Jo Mae. Jo Mae wasn't waiting in any line for a turn. She was just standing uncertainly in the middle of the court.

Sharon bent forward to take a good look at the left side of Jo Mae's shirt. I walked in front of Sharon's face. "See, I told you it didn't have a tear in it."

Before Sharon could figure out if the shirt had been mended, I pushed Jo Mae toward an empty pole. "Come on and play a game with me. Nobody's on this one."

Maybe they don't play tetherball in the South where Jo Mae used to live. She caught on fast, though. By the time recess was over, she could wham the ball hard and keep it going above my head. She leaped up in the air a couple of times on the way back to the building. "You can sure jump higher in Nikes than you can in boots," she said.

Lester and Jack were behind me when I went into our room. "My sister made sugar cookies once," Lester was telling Jack. "Only she made a mistake and used salt instead of sugar. That'd make a nice gift for Sharon."

Greedy Eyes

On Saturday evening, I put on my best blouse and joined Dad in the living room. "You look handsome," I told him. He looked *too* handsome, I thought. Brittany's mother was sure to be impressed.

He bent down and kissed me. "Thank you very much."

"And you smell good, too." It was the clean smell of his fresh, shaved face that I liked.

As we walked down the hall to Brittany's apartment, I tried to be happy. This was better than having my dad spend the evening staring sadly at his newspaper.

"Come in. Come in," Mrs. James said at her apartment door. She had her big smile on and a purple and blue cotton dress that came down to the floor.

"I like your dress," I said politely.

"This old caftan. I always wear it when I cook for company because it doesn't show any splatters."

Brittany came in the living room with a tray of drinks. She passed the tray to Dad, her mother, and then to me. She took the last glass and sat beside me on the davenport. Our parents sat on fuzzy, peach-colored chairs.

Mrs. James saw me looking at the walls that matched the chairs. "Do you like the paint job?" she asked.

"Sure beats our brown walls," I said.

"I hated those depressing, gloomy rooms. Before we even moved our furniture in, I was up on a ladder painting and had Brittany doing the trim."

Brittany made a face at me. "It took a whole week."

"I bet it did," Dad said. "The place looks great."

Mrs. James seemed pleased with herself.

"Do you like the drink?" Brittany asked me.

"It's very good."

"All you do is put orange juice in the blender with some frozen strawberries. It comes out pink and frosty."

It was good, all right. The dinner was, too. Fried chicken and mashed potatoes and green beans with toasted almonds sprinkled on top. When we came to the blackberry pie, I was almost enjoying myself. Then Brittany brought up my mom's jewelry.

"You know," she said, looking at her mother, "Marianne has a whole box of stuff. Earrings and beads and rings."

"That must be fun when you play dress-up." Mrs. James didn't need to smile at me so sweetly. Nobody plays dress-up in the fourth grade.

"She has the neatest ring. I'd sure like a ring with a red stone." Brittany's dark eyes were squinted into greedy slits.

"Well," Mrs. James said, "maybe if you share something with Marianne, she'll share some of what she has with you."

I looked at my father for help. He was quietly forking up the last bite of his pie.

"Let me get you another piece," Mrs. James suggested to him.

Dad held up his hand. "No, no. That was just right. It was the best meal I've had in months."

"Anytime," she said with raised eyebrows.

He smiled back at her and the whole thing made me so sick I couldn't even think of being happy for him.

I got even sicker after dinner when Brittany took me into her room. She went straight to her dresser and began pawing through her top drawer. She pulled out a black beaded purse. "Isn't this neat?" she asked me.

I shrugged. "What's it for?"

"My grandma gave it to me. She took it with her

when she went dancing. Do you like it?"

"I guess so," I said.

"You can have it."

"No thanks. You keep it, if it's from your grand-
mother."

"No, I want to give it to you." She shoved the purse
at me.

I backed away. She wanted to give it to me, I knew,
so she could have my mom's ring.

"Go on. Take it," she insisted.

"No. My dad said you aren't supposed to give away
presents."

"Well. Well, that's stupid. Everything we have was
a present once."

I stood there with my hands at my sides, trying to be
sure I didn't make things worse. "Do you have a game
we can play?"

"Sure, I've got some games. Do you want a game?"
She threw the purse down on her bed and dived into
the bottom of her closet.

"I . . . I didn't mean to keep. I meant to play."

She didn't pay attention to what I was saying. She
was too busy throwing out dirty clothes and old shoes.
The crushed box of a Monopoly game was in her hand
when she crawled out of the mess. "Hey, how about
this?"

Mrs. James opened the bedroom door. "Oh, were you two just starting to play?"

"No. No! We were just talking. Is my dad ready to go?" I hurried past her and out to the living room.

I stayed close to my dad while I thanked Mrs. James for the delicious dinner and thanked Brittany, too, for having us over.

On the way back to our apartment, Dad said, "I think you'd better put your mother's jewel box away. It's too much of a temptation for your friends."

"Don't worry," I told him. "I'll hide it good."

Miss Jewell zeroed in on Jack right after she took roll on Monday morning. "Did you think of something nice that you could do for Sharon?"

"Yes," he said, "I brought something. I'll give it to her at lunch."

When she heard that, a smile turned up Sharon's lips. She exchanged secret glances with Lindsey. I hoped what Jack had for her wasn't salted cookies or he'd be in trouble again.

During reading, I started up a daydream about my mom. Mrs. James's face kept jumping into my head, though. I didn't want to picture her. I didn't even want to live near her. What if I got Brittany for a stepsister?

Miss Jewell's hand was on my shoulder, giving it a

sharp shake. "Marianne! Sit up and get to work."

The look she gave me was stern. No more gentle words about being sad for me. Miss Jewell meant business. I picked up my card and tried to concentrate on question six.

At lunchtime, Jack took two sacks to his seat. He peeked in the smaller one, pulled out a cupcake, walked across the room, and plunked it down on Sharon's desk. "I'm sorry I hit you with spit wads."

Before Sharon could say a word, he beetled back to his desk. Miss Jewell nodded towards him. "That was very nice, Jack."

Sharon looked down at her cupcake. The chocolate frosting was smashed over the sides. She frowned as she pushed it back over the top. I watched her until she licked the frosting off her finger. She didn't screech so I guessed it was OK.

After I'd eaten my sandwich, Jack turned around. He was munching on a cupcake. He held another one out to me. "I brought three," he said. "I made them myself."

The frosting on my cupcake was a bit messy, but it hadn't gotten smashed down in the sack. I took a big bite of it quick, before Sharon could spot the difference between hers and mine.

At recess, Sharon must have told some of the kids

in the other fourth grade room that Jack gave her a cupcake. Leon kept darting up to him on the playground. "Jack's got a new girl. Jack likes Sharon."

Jack swatted at him and Leon danced away. "Jack likes Sharon."

Sharon was watching from the tetherball court, trying to hide a smile behind her hand. Leon sang out again, "Jack likes Sharon."

This time Jack grabbed Leon by the shirt and yanked him around in a circle. "Shut up or I'll shut you up!"

Mrs. Wilson swooped down on them. "Jack, you go sit on the bench."

Jack dropped Leon's shirt and moved away towards the bench, mumbling, "Well, tell him to shut his face."

"Hey," Leon called after him, "I can't help it if you . . ."

"Leon," Mrs. Wilson ordered, "keep quiet and go stand by the wall."

"I only said . . ."

"Go stand by the wall!"

Leon did.

For the rest of lunch recess, I swung on the bars with Jenny and Diane. Sharon and Lindsey walked around the playground, whispering. Jack sat slumped on the bench.

The Fight

I walked partway home with Jo Mae after school. She was hoping and hoping her dad would find a job pretty soon. "It's really packed at my grandma's," she said.

"I bet," I agreed.

"Where do you live?" she asked me.

"About four blocks down in an old apartment building. We just moved there so I could stay in the same school until Dad finds us a new house. I wouldn't hate the place so much, but there's a girl there who bothers me."

Jo Mae slowed her steps and looked closely into my face. She has pretty, light-blue eyes, but I think she must be nearsighted. "Can't you just keep away from that girl?"

"No." I shook my head. "She gets home before I do and waits for me at my door."

"You only have one door?"

I came to a full stop on the sidewalk. "Wow, you're right. I can go in the back way!" I wanted to hug Jo Mae, I was so relieved. Instead I tapped her on the shoulder. "Thanks. I don't know why I didn't think of that."

She kicked at a small rock, smiling shyly. "I know how you feel. I don't like that ol' Sharon much."

"She can be real nosey."

"Well," Jo Mae said. "This is my grandma's street."

I said good-bye to her, then ran three blocks, turned, and slipped down the alley. I passed the garbage cans, went through the metal service door, and climbed the concrete stairs. Up in our kitchen, I took in a few big breaths to get my wind back.

I wasn't as depressed as I usually am when I get home. Dad had bought some gingersnaps. I took the box of them in the living room, pushed the footstool close to the TV, and turned it on real low. There was an after-school special on. It was about a couple of kids who were trying to save their grandpa from being put in a nursing home.

Most of the time, I switched the sound off at the

commercial. When I did, I could hear Brittany shuffling against the front door. Once I didn't turn the sound off. I was thinking, Why don't the kids just take turns caring for their grandpa so their mother wouldn't feel he was too big of a burden for her?

While I was wondering this, a man in a used-car commercial blasted out, "Come in and see Uncle Denny! He'll give you the best deal in town!"

There was loud knocking at my door. Oh, oh! I switched the sound off and huddled down on the footstool. The knocking turned to banging.

I put the remote control back on top of the TV. The kids in the movie were stupid anyway. I crept out of the living room and into my bedroom and stayed there until Brittany finally gave up.

The next day after school, I came in the back way again. This time, though, I read my library book and left the TV off. That night Dad took me to McDonald's for Chicken McDLT's.

We had barely gotton home when there were more knocks at the door. My stomach told me it would be Brittany and her mother. It was.

Dad let them in. Mrs. James was carrying another blackberry pie oozing with dark red juice. "I just took this pie out of the oven," she said gaily. "And I thought it might be fun to share it with you people."

We ate the pie on the rickety table in the kitchen. Dad apologized for our lack of furniture. "We sold ours with the house," he told Mrs. James.

A bitter look crossed Mrs. James's face. "My ex-husband kept all of ours. And the house, too."

"But he gave us money for new furniture," Brittany said.

"He didn't have much of a choice." Mrs. James pushed her black hair back from her face and then focused on me. "Have you been sick, Marianne?"

"No," I said.

She raised her eyebrows. "Just playing hookey?"

"No," I said.

"Well, Brittany tells me she doesn't see you come home from school. But she hears the TV playing inside the apartment."

Dad put down his fork and looked at me, too.

I stared from face to face, trying to get my courage up. "Sometimes I come in the back way."

"Why do you do that?" Mrs. James's voice was sharp.

At first I wasn't going to answer her. But, finally, when the silence got heavy, I murmured, "Sometimes I don't feel like playing with anybody."

"Why didn't you just tell Brittany that? Don't you think it's unkind to let her wait and wait and wait for you?"

I kept my eyes focused on my half-eaten pie as I nodded my head.

To my relief, Dad took over then. "We've had some troubles adjusting . . . "

"Oh, yes, of course. Of course," Mrs. James's voice had turned sugary again.

"Perhaps," Dad went on, "when Marianne feels like having company, she could go down to your apartment to ask Brittany if she wants to play."

"Oh. Oh. I guess that would be fine." Mrs. James seemed taken aback for a minute. "But, the only thing is . . . I did think it was comforting to know the girls were together when we couldn't be with them."

"I call Marianne every afternoon," Dad explained, "to be sure she's home and to be sure she's all right."

"Yes, but that isn't quite the same . . . Well, I do understand that you won't be yourselves for a while. I just wonder if isolating yourselves is the answer." She turned her wide smile on Brittany. "Well, dear, it's about time for you to be getting at your homework."

Dad saw them to the door. I sat at the table wondering if he liked Mrs. James and if I was messing up his chances of having fun with her. My dad never says mean things about people so it's hard to tell what he feels about them.

"Do you like Mrs. James?" I asked him when he came back in the kitchen.

"She makes good pies," he said.

She did that all right.

At school the other fourth grade class was still teasing Jack about giving Sharon a cupcake. They didn't know Miss Jewell made him or that I had one, too. Leon was the worst heckler. He wouldn't let up on Jack.

Most kids like Jack. Miss Jewell reminds him that he's a natural leader when she's trying to get him to behave. She tells him other kids follow him and he should try to set an example. It is kind of hard to set an example when someone rushes up to you and pokes you and says you like Sharon Hinkler.

Leon did that for three days, until Jack had really had it. It was at noon recess that he grabbed Leon by the shirt again. This time he didn't just yank him around. He threw Leon on the ground and jumped on top of him.

All the kids gathered around in a circle to watch. I kept one eye on the fight and one eye on Mrs. Wilson who was busy scolding a fifth grader over by the wall. She wasn't noticing the crowd cheering the fight on. That was good, too, because Jack was pounding three days of being mad into Leon's face.

"You can just shut up about me and Hinkler," Jack snarled, smashing Leon in the mouth again.

"OK. OK." Leon was panting and squirming and trying to get out from under Jack.

"You sure you're going to remember?" Jack held his fist over Leon's head.

"Ya, I'm sure." Leon had his arm over his bloody nose to ward off any more blows.

"Jack, Jack!" I edged inside the circle and pulled at his sweater. "Jack, Mrs. Wilson's coming."

He got up quick. Leon got up, too. Not soon enough, though. Mrs. Wilson took them both by their necks and marched them off to the principal's office.

Jack didn't come back to the room after recess was over. He didn't come back all afternoon. Every time our classroom door opened, I looked around to see if it was Jack. It never was.

After school, I went into the office to see if he was there. He and Leon were sitting in chairs outside the principal's door. "What's going on?" I wanted to know.

Jack tilted his head toward the closed door. "Our moms are in there."

"Will she be real mad?" I asked.

"Naw, she's used to it."

"Mine will kill me," Leon said.

You Gotta Do the Work

The next morning, Jack was in his seat before I was. "What happened?" I asked him as I settled down.

"Not much," he said.

"But what?"

"Well, my mom told me not to be so sensitive about being teased. She knows Mrs. Hinkler and Mrs. Hinkler's a pain just like Sharon, and you can't get upset by people like that."

"Didn't Mr. Douglas do anything?"

"He gave me a big lecture about setting goals and talked to me about all the things I could do in the school if I became a Master Wizard."

"That's all?"

"No. He said if I get in another fight, he'll send me home for three days." Jack's eyes shifted to the side for a few seconds, before he slowly looked back at me. "I heard something else. I'll tell you about it at lunchtime."

"OK," I agreed. "But do you want to be a Master Wizard?"

"Hmmm. Maybe. It'd be neat to be on the stage crew."

I guessed it would be neat. I figured I'd never make it. I daydreamed too much. When I put my head down that day, though, Jack turned around and ordered, "Sit up!"

I did. And every time I forgot, he turned around again. I don't know how he knew when my head went down. He had never talked mean to me before, and about the third time, I asked, "Why?"

"I said I'd tell you at lunch," he whispered.

At lunchtime, he scooted his chair around to my desk. Between bites of his egg-salad sandwiches, he told me that when Mrs. Wilson had left Leon and him outside the principal's door, he heard Mr. Douglas and Miss Jewell talking inside the principal's office. Miss Jewell was saying that she didn't know what to do with me. She said I was a nice girl and she understood that I might be lost without my mother, but that I wasn't doing any work.

"You gotta do the work," Jack told me.

"I know," I said.

"What do you do when you get home from school?"

"There's nothing to do. Nothing I like, anyway."

"You need a dog," Jack decided. Then he bit his upper lip in thought. "A wolf hybrid."

"A wolf?"

"Half a wolf. They're half wolf and half dog. They're real smart. My uncle has one. I want one, but my brother already has a spaniel and my mom says that's as much as she can put up with."

A wolf. I thought I'd love a wolf. Even half of a wolf. "Oh," I said, imagining putting my arms around a big, furry ruff, "I'd like to have a wolf."

"They're real cool," Jack said. "Ask your dad tonight. Wolves have puppies in the spring. So you should be able to get one now."

"Where do you get one?" I wanted to know.

"Look in the ads in the newspaper. That's what my uncle did."

Lester came up to us then and bumped Jack's leg with his knee. "Check out the clock."

"Oops, recess time." Jack wadded up his sandwich wrappings and stuffed them inside his lunch sack. "Come on," he said to me. "The contest starts today. We have to go to the gym and jump. I wanna win a camera."

The Heart Association got the money the sponsors donated for each minute we jumped, but there were prizes for the students who brought in the most money. Like, if you brought in $25, you got a kite. If you brought in $50, you got a T-shirt with a red heart on it. If you brought in $100, you got a jacket and a glow rope. And if you brought in $400, you got a camera. There were other prizes, too, but Jack was zeroed in on the camera. His big brother, Kevin, had one, but Kevin wouldn't let Jack touch it.

The only sponsor I had was my dad, so I couldn't win anything. I just went along with Jack. I was following dreamily after him and Lester, when Jenny caught up with me at the gym door. "What were you talking about at lunch?"

"Jack was telling me about wolf-dogs," I said. "He thinks one would keep me company."

"Or eat you up," she suggested.

"No, wolves are real nice," I said.

I explained that again to my dad when he got home from work. "They're intelligent, too," I told him.

"I'm sure they are," he said, "but we can't have one in an apartment."

"I thought we were going to move pretty soon." I

was sitting next to him on the davenport and I pushed down the lumpy springs in one of the cushions. "And leave this old thing behind."

He nodded. "I guess it's past time all right. I'll tell you what. I'll call a real-estate office tomorrow. After we get a house, we'll talk about a dog."

"Half a dog," I corrected him.

"Hmmm. We'll see." He gave me a teasing grin. "But are you sure you wouldn't rather have a tiger?"

"Very funny," I said.

Later in bed, I didn't think it was so funny. I really *would* like to have a tiger. Next best was a wolf hybrid.

It took two Saturdays and Sundays of looking before the real-estate man started to get impatient. "This house is near your school and it's got a good-size yard." He glanced at Dad and then at me. "The couple who owns it are getting a divorce. Otherwise you'd never get a rec room and three bedrooms in your price range."

The last thing I wanted was three bedrooms. Brittany hadn't been bothering me lately, but I didn't want to take any chances of having a house big enough for her and her mother.

"Well, kitten?" Dad said. "It seems fine to me."

We were standing on the front lawn, looking out at the sidewalk. The three bedrooms weren't all that worried me. The yard really wasn't large enough. Jack said a wolf hybrid has to have lots of room to run and hunt mice.

I could feel the real-estate man frowning while he waited for my answer. "The place is neat," I mumbled, "but the yard's too little."

"Too little?" His voice boomed in my ears. "It's seventy-five feet by a hundred feet. That's almost twice as big as an average lot."

"I know." I kept my head down so he couldn't see my face. "But it's still too little."

He sighed. "Well, let's go back to the office and check on any new listings that might have come in."

Dad and I stood beside the man's desk while he clicked at his computer and then thumbed through a big note-book. About halfway into the notebook, he held a page out to us. "There is this little cottage on one and a third acres that's also in Brier. It's only four rooms and a bath. The living room is extra large, though, and it has a stone fireplace."

A stone fireplace. An acre and a third. Joy bubbled up inside me as Dad and I peered at the picture of a one-story house with a wide porch all around it. Flowers were climbing over one side of the porch.

"Does it have two bedrooms?"Dad asked.

"Yes," the man said.

"Is that enough?" I was watching Dad's face closely.

He smiled down at me. "I don't think we need any more, do we?"

I hoped not.

When the real-estate man pulled up in front of the house, we stayed in the car a minute looking at it. The flowers growing over the porch were roses. Mom had a rose garden.

The sad, heavy feeling came down over me again. My dad sat quietly in the front seat. The real-estate man must have thought we didn't like the house. "Do you want to see the inside?"

"Sure," my dad said and we got out of the car.

Before we went up the porch steps, the man pointed at the roses. "They're Climbing Royal Sunsets. They're fine plants. Hardy and everblooming."

"My mom had a red rose growing over the fence by our old house. She said it was called Blaze."

"Climbing Blaze is attractive." The man broke off a flower and handed it to me. "But smell this."

The flower had the colors of a sunset, pink and peach and yellow. It smelled delicious.

In the living room, I ran my hand over the big, rough stones of the fireplace. "This room smells good, too," I said.

The man nodded. "That's the cedar boards on the

walls. They'll smell good forever." The wood walls were a soft golden color. Not a bit like the ugly, brown plaster in the smelly apartment.

I went outside to check out the yard while the real-estate man and Dad checked out the plumbing and the house's foundation. There were fruit trees way in the back and a little building.

I pushed open the door made out of wooden slats. The floor was made of cement. The place looked like a small barn. Perfect for a wolf-dog, I thought. And as I imagined him there, my sadness slipped away.

When I returned to the house, the man explained that the building had been used for goats. It'd seemed a bit goaty, all right. "I'll have to scrub it out for Kipluck," I told my dad.

"Oh?" He raised his eyebrows. "So you've already named your wolf and moved him in."

The real-estate man looked startled for a minute. "A wolf?" Then he put his beaming-salesman face back on and asked Dad, "Well, do we have a deal?"

"I think so," my dad said.

Half a Wolf

Usually we jumped for the Jump-a-thon only at recess. But because this Monday was the last day of the contest, we were allowed in the gym before school. Tom, Lester, and I were at the gym doors before Mr. Douglas even had them opened. I was surprised Jack wasn't there.

As soon as the kids were inside, everyone grabbed for a single rope. Mr. Douglas started the music and we all started jumping. When two minutes were up, he turned off the music and recorded the names of the jumpers. Then he started the music again. I was getting pretty pooped by the time Jack and Jenny showed up.

Jack looked like he was trying not to cry. Especially

when he saw there were no more single ropes. I dropped mine and picked up one of the long ones. "Here, Jenny," I said, "take the other end."

We got the rope swinging and Jack hopped in just as the music began again. Jenny and I kept swinging and Jack kept jumping until the first bell rang and Mr. Douglas hollered out, "That does it!"

After Jack had his name checked off, he and Jenny and I walked to our room together. He still looked miserable. "So much for a camera."

"You'll win something, though," Jenny told him.

"Yeah, a stupid glow rope or jogging shorts."

"I'd like a glow rope," I said.

"If I get one, you can have it." He let out a long sigh. "I asked my mom to give me the alarm clock. But she said no, Dad needed it and she'd be sure to wake me up."

"She forgot?" Jenny asked.

"She forgot," Jack said.

I was dying to tell him about the new house, but he felt so bad I thought I'd better wait. By lunchtime he'd feel better, I figured.

He started eating all by himself. Most days he moved over to sit with Lester. Sometimes he ate with me. Especially if Jenny and the other Master Wizards were invited to eat with the principal.

I chewed on my peanut butter sandwich until I couldn't wait any longer. "Jack, Jack!" I poked him on the shoulder.

"What, what?" he said and turned around.

"We bought a house. With an acre and a third. And it's empty so we get to move in and rent until the bank papers are signed."

"Awright!" Jack said. "I'll call my uncle tonight and find out where he got his wolf-dog."

I told Jo Mae, too, when I caught up with her after school. She was already smiling because her dad had found work. "It's just a little ol' night watchman's job," she explained. "We can't buy a house yet, but Mama's trying to find something to rent near our school."

"Don't let her get a place in my smelly building," I warned her.

When I got to the apartment, Brittany was hanging around the alley. She followed me in the back door. I was feeling so good I didn't even get upset when she went on following me right into my bedroom. As I hung up my jacket, I could see her looking over my dresser.

"Where's that jewel box?" she asked.

"My dad told me to put it away."

"Why? What's the matter with playing with it?"

"Dad would rather we didn't. Let's go in the living room to watch TV."

She didn't have much choice but to come in the living room, too. When she sat down on the davenport, she picked up the *Consumer Reports Buying Guide Issue* that Dad had left there. "What's this for?" she wanted to know.

"We're getting a new refrigerator and stove."

"You could sure use some new stuff . . ." She stopped talking mean suddenly, as if she were remembering something. "We've got enough furniture for two families."

I didn't answer her. I just kept switching the TV programs, trying to find something better than cartoons for four-year-olds.

"Oh, I almost forgot," Brittany said loudly. "Mom and I are going to the science center Saturday afternoon and she thought you and your dad would like to come along."

I turned the TV off. "We can't."

"Why not?"

"Because we're moving Saturday." I watched her eyes get big.

"Moving? You're moving? Where?"

"In a house."

"Where? Around here?"

"Oh, about a mile away, I guess. On an acre and a third. The real-estate man said the lady next door has a horse. I'm going to get a wolf hybrid."

"You mean one of those half-wolf, half-dog animals? I heard someone on TV say those are dangerous because they can turn wild on you."

"I hope so," I told her. "I like wild wolves."

At school the next morning, Jack handed me a slip of paper with a phone number and the name "Mrs. Thompson" written on it. "Call that lady," Jack said. "My uncle thinks she should have some puppies now. He got his last May."

"What color are they?"

"White," he said.

"*White?*"

"Sure," he said. "They're half artic wolf and half Samoyed."

The last bell rang and Miss Jewell stood in front of the room waiting for our attention. Jack had to turn around. While Miss Jewell took roll. I sat there feeling itchy with disappointment. I had expected a gray and black wolf like the girl had in the movie *The Journey of Natty Gann*. Not a white one. My wolf-dog could have white legs and a white belly, but not be all white.

That night Dad brought home fish and chips. He wanted lots of time after dinner to pack kitchen stuff like canned food, flour, baking powder, and cinnamon and syrup. While we ate, I read through the pet ads in the paper. There were three inches of ads for free kittens, but none for wolf hybrids.

"I had a border collie when I was a kid," my dad said. "They're good dogs."

"I want a wolf-dog," I said.

There were still none advertised on Tuesday or Wednesday or Thursday. "Wait till Sunday," Dad advised me. "There are a lot more ads then."

But I didn't have to wait until Sunday. Friday night there were two ads. The first one said, "WOLF HYBRIDS 8 wks old. Remarkably intelligent, healthy, make loving companions." The number to call was Mrs. Thompson's.

The second ad said, "Wolf-mix. 6 wks old. 5 females, 2 males."

"That's it," I told Dad. "I'll call right now."

"Hold on. You haven't filled up those cartons I put in your room. The appliance men will be at the house at eleven tomorrow morning with the stove and refrigerator. So we have to have the U-Haul trailer packed and over there by then. So get crackin'."

"I will. I will," I promised him. "I'll just call and see what the puppies are like."

I was dialing the phone before he could say no. But when the man at the other end said, "Hello," I couldn't think of what to ask.

"Um . . . um, you have puppies?"

"Yes," the man said.

"Well, um, what are they like?"

"Oh, they're brownish-gray and pretty lively."

That sounded good. "What's the mother and father like?"

"She's a German shepherd. My wife knows a little more about the father. She was visiting her sister when a neighbor's animal got to our dog. My wife said he looked like a gray wolf."

"Thank you." I put the phone down slowly and went to find my dad. He'd gone into his bedroom to finish emptying his drawers.

"The man said the puppies' father 'looked like a gray wolf.' "

"Well, you can *look* at the puppies after we're moved and after we're settled in the new house."

"Sunday," I said and dashed for my bedroom before he could tell me to get crackin' again.

My dad is slow to get started. But once he gets going, he wants to "do it right." Doing it "right" meant that hauling our stuff into the new house from the trailer was only the beginning.

Sunday morning, I had to wash the insides of all the kitchen and bathroom cupboards while he cut the paper to line them. Only then could we unpack the boxes and put things away.

When he'd burned the last of the packing material

in the fireplace and I'd finished sweeping, I begged, "Please, can we go look at puppies now?"

"Aren't you hungry?" he asked. "I am."

"Let's get a hamburger on the way," I pleaded.

Even though we'd gone shopping Saturday night and the new refrigerator was full of food, he tilted his head down, rolled his eyes up, and said, "We-ell, I guess we could do that."

Finally! I grabbed the phone to call the man with the wolf-mix puppies for his address. After I'd gotten it, Dad said, "You'd better call that Mrs. Thompson for her address, too. Just in case."

So I did.

Curved Fangs and Claws

The wolf-mix puppies lived in a neighborhood of shabby houses and tiny yards. I looked down at the broken boards on the porch as Dad rang the bell. This didn't seem to be a very good home for animals.

The man I had talked to on the phone let us in. He took us through the messy house and into the backyard. Out there was a skinny police dog with a bunch of grayish-brown puppies running after her. They were all trying to get at her belly for a drink of milk. She kept pulling away from them, but the fenced-in area was so small she couldn't get very far.

I felt sorry for the mother dog. She looked worn-out.

"Do you have a picture of the father?" I asked the man.

"No, I don't. My sister-in-law said her neighbor told her he was part gray wolf."

Only a part, I thought. That would make the puppies less than half. The front doorbell rang and the man left us to let some more people in. I whispered to Dad that I didn't think the puppies looked very wolfish. He whispered back that he didn't think the mother dog looked very healthy.

When the man brought a lady and a boy out to the dirt yard, my dad thanked him for showing us his dogs. We went back to the car and found Mrs. Thompson's address on our map. On the ride there, I tried to picture a white wolf in my mind.

Mrs. Thompson lived way out in the country. When we turned off the Machias road, we passed an old-fashioned church. "Look at that." I pointed out the window. "It has a steeple with a bell."

Mrs. Thompson's place wasn't far from the church. Dad parked the car outside the fence. A huge, white wolf-dog with slanted eyes jumped at the gate as my dad tried to push it open. A gray-haired woman hurried down the long path from the house. "Come on in," she called. "He's friendly."

He might be too friendly, I thought. He could easily knock you flat on your back. As we went through the gate, I sort of edged away from him.

"Stay down, Aluke!" she ordered the dog. He minded her, but I could see he still wanted to jump on someone. Instead he loped around Mrs. Thompson while she took us over to another slant-eyed wolf-dog who was stretched out in the shade of a cedar tree. Some furry, fat puppies were sleeping in a pile beside her. One was tugging at the end of her fluffy tail. Two others were wrestling in the grass.

The mother dog didn't get mad at the puppy pulling her tail. She just reached around and pushed him away with her nose. It was then Aluke crouched down on his two front legs and the puppy dashed to attack him. Aluke whirled away with the fat puppy scrambling after him.

I sat on the grass and petted one of the sleeping puppies. It stirred awake and crawled towards a nipple. The mother wolf-dog gave a low growl. The puppy decided to chew on my sandals instead.

"She makes them mind," I said.

"Oh, yes," Mrs. Thompson agreed. "When she decides it's time for them to be weaned, they're weaned."

"Ow!" I yelled. "Cut that out." I tried to pry the puppy's jaw open to save my toe. Its teeth were caught in my sock.

Mrs. Thompson sat down beside me, unhooked the

puppy's tooth, turned up its lip, and showed me its needle-sharp fangs. "See, the fangs are curved," she explained. She pressed on the puppy's paw with her fingers, making its toes spread out. "See, he has claws instead of toenails. He'll naturally want to put up his paws when he plays with you. He doesn't know the claws can rip your skin. You have to teach a wolf hybrid to keep his paws down."

My dad kneeled on the grass in front of me. "Are you sure this is what you want?"

"I'm sure." I looked at Dad and then at Mrs. Thompson. "I could train one, couldn't I?"

"Of course, but you don't make pets of them quite the way you do dogs. They are more your friends. They try to understand what you want and you try to understand what they want. If they make a mistake and wet on the rug, you pick them up immediately, say 'No' in a loud voice, and put them out on the ground. You never hit them. They wouldn't hurt you. If you hurt them, they can decide they don't want you for a friend."

I stared at Mrs. Thompson in horror. "Oh, I would never, never hurt one."

She leaned over and stroked the mother wolf-dog's head. "What kind of a puppy were you looking for? A playful one, a bossy one, a male, a female?"

While I thought that over, I watched Aluke who was

far out in the yard. He was crouched down again, waiting for the panting puppy to catch up to him. "Well," I told Mrs. Thompson, "at first I imagined one like the girl had in a movie I saw . . ."

"One more like a malamute? Whitehawk's mother was part malamute." Whitehawk raised her front leg so Mrs. Thompson could scratch under her chest.

"We understood they were half arctic wolf and half Samoyed," my dad said.

"Aluke is. Whitehawk is arctic and malamute."

"How come she's so light?" I asked.

"I wanted a female to match Aluke, so I picked out the lightest one in the litter." Mrs. Thompson stopped scratching Whitehawk and pulled a puppy out of the bottom of the sleeping pile. "This one is the darkest in this litter." She handed me a puppy with gray shading down his back and around his face. "He has a pretty mask."

I took the puppy in my arms. He opened his almond eyes, stretched up, and licked my chin with his little pink tongue. "Ohhh, Kipluck," I crooned.

Mrs. Thompson and Dad both laughed. I didn't care. I just hugged my puppy tighter.

The ride home scared Kipluck. He spent most of it with his head burrowed under my arm. Just as Dad parked in front of our house, I saw a lady with blonde hair flying behind her come down the road on a galloping horse.

After we climbed out of the car, she pulled up the horse beside us. "What have you got there?" she asked me. "Look at those slanted eyes. It's part wolf, isn't it?"

"Yes," I told her proudly, "he's a wolf hybrid."

She leaned over the side of her horse and peered into Kipluck's face. "What color are his eyes going to be?"

I shifted Kipluck around in my arms. He was heavy and my arms were getting tired. "His mother's eyes were yellow and his father's eyes were brown. The woman we bought him from said puppies' eyes are blue when they're born."

"They look muddy-green about now," Dad said.

"Bring your puppy over to see me one of these days," the lady invited. "I'm Lacy."

"I'm Marianne."

"And I'm Jim," Dad said.

We were all smiling at each other when a car drove up behind the horse. Lacy clacked her tongue twice. The horse broke into a trot, turned at the house next door, and went around to the barn in back.

"What a neat neighbor," I said to my dad. The way he was still smiling made me think he thought so, too.

There was a honk from the car, which hadn't moved.

I turned to look at it. Rats! Brittany and Mrs. James were inside.

They got out of the car and took a picnic basket from the trunk. "I thought maybe you two would enjoy a home-cooked meal in the midst of your moving," Mrs. James said. She and Brittany lugged the basket into our yard.

I put Kipluck down. He sniffed around the grass and then squatted to pee. "Oh, it's cute." Brittany reached out to Kipluck. He backed up to me and let out a growl.

"He doesn't know you," I explained. "And you have to be careful how you play with him because he has claws and fangs."

Mrs. James's big smile dropped from her face. "What kind of dog is he?"

"He's a wolf hybrid," I told her.

She looked at my dad with alarm. "Is that safe for a little girl?"

"I guess we'll see," he said.

I rolled Kipluck over and rubbed his fat, pink tummy. Brittany stood uncertainly beside me. "Well? Well? How do you play with him?"

"Easy," I said. I got a dead branch from under one of our apple trees and dragged the tip along the ground. Kipluck pounced on it. I pulled from my end. Kipluck sank his teeth in the wood and pulled from his end.

When the branch broke, Kipluck dashed away with his piece. I chased after him, grabbed at the stick, and tugged it free. I sat on the ground whirling the branch around me while he ran after it. After a while he crouched down and just watched the stick going around and around.

I had to shift hands behind me to make the full circle each time. As I slowed to shift, Kipluck zipped in back of me and caught the branch. "See how smart he is?" I said to my dad. "He figured out how to get it."

My dad nodded. Mrs. James seemed a little bored. "I understand you have a new refrigerator and stove. Shall we put the casserole in the oven?"

"Sure." Dad picked up the basket and headed for the house. "But that's about all we have inside."

"Well, that's about all you need. For a while." She was looking up into his face as she walked beside him. Yuck, I thought to myself.

Brittany isn't the kind of girl who can stay out of the action for long. "Here. Let me play with the puppy now." She undid the belt from around her waist and dangled it above Kipluck.

Kipluck dropped the branch and went after the belt.

"Be careful," I warned. "He might put scratches on it."

"Oh, it's old." She was bending from her waist with

her head pointed towards Kipluck while she held her arm up in the air.

"Be careful of his claws," I warned again, but Brittany isn't the kind of girl who listens to you.

She jerked the belt up and down. Kipluck jumped for it. "Watch out . . ." I started to say just as Kipluck's paw hit Brittany's mouth. His sharp claw raked her lower lip as he bounced back to the ground.

Blood poured down Brittany's chin. She let go of the belt and clapped her hand over her mouth. When she took her hand away and saw the blood, she screamed, "Mama!"

Slower Than a Slug

An hour and a half went by before Brittany and her mother returned from the hospital emergency room. I expected Brittany to have stitches on her lip. She didn't have to have any, but she did have to have a tetanus shot. That was so she wouldn't get an infection from the wolf claws, Brittany explained. "And I don't think much of your dog," she added.

"How much was the bill?" my dad asked quietly.

"Eighty dollars," Mrs. James said, handing him her receipt.

Dad sat down at our card table and wrote out a check.

When he handed it to her, Mrs. James took it slowly. "I don't know if you should be paying all of this. After all, Brittany was playing with the dog."

"The pup is our responsibility," he said firmly.

I stood in the middle of the kitchen feeling awful. My dad had told me not to worry. Accidents like this could happen with any puppy. I still felt awful, though. Especially about the money. After he made the house down payment, Dad had said we had just enough savings left for our furniture.

Kipluck had cost a hundred and fifty dollars. The hospital cost eighty dollars. And there were still puppy shots and wire fencing to buy.

I looked at Kipluck sleeping in the corner of the kitchen. He was curled into a furry ball with his closed eyes making slanted lines toward his nose. I knew I could feel better if I held him in my lap and loved him. But puppies need their naps.

"Well, shall we put the casserole back in the oven?" Mrs. James suggested with a bright smile. "I'm hungry. Aren't the rest of you hungry, too?"

I didn't feel much like eating. I sort of picked at my food. Brittany ate plenty—between big fusses about how bad it made her lip hurt.

I was relieved when they left. Before Dad and I got the dishes done, Kipluck woke up. I hurried him out to the yard. When he squatted in the grass, I told him, "Good Kipluck! That's a good boy!"

He wasn't such a good boy in the middle of the night. But that was my fault. He tried.

Dad said the pup could stay in the house just for the first night. After that, he would have to sleep out on the porch. Wolf hybrids need to be in the cold to grow their heavy coats of fur.

I put an old blanket in the corner of the kitchen and sat on it. Kipluck immediately climbed on my lap. I played tug-of-war with him and rubbed his tummy until he was sleepy. But when I got up to sneak off to bed, his eyes popped open.

Every time he trotted after me, I put him on his blanket and told him to stay. He whimpered a bit, but he finally gave up, lay down with his head on his paws, and watched me sadly as I went to my room without him.

It seemed like I was barely asleep when Kipluck's whines woke me up. I took him outside and shivered in the night air while he sniffed around for a place to pee. It must have been past midnight when he cried again. I shoved my feet into my slippers, hurried to the kitchen, opened the door, carried him down the steps, and set him on the grass. Just in time.

Back in the house, he scampered around, ready to play. I was groggy, but I petted him awhile, anyway, and then told him to stay on his blanket. I wasn't even asleep before he whined some more. I decided he was lonesome and would have to get used to sleeping without his brothers and sisters. He howled, but I still didn't get up. I was sure he didn't have to go again so soon.

In the morning, Kipluck greeted me with hops and jumps at my legs. His sharp claws pricked through my jeans. "No, no," I told him, "that hurts."

Before I picked him up to take him outside, I sniffed. And sniffed again. There was a bad smell in the house.

After I brought Kipluck inside, I went into the living room. A brown pile was in the middle of the rug. How dense can you get, I told myself. I had forgotten all about his having to do that, too.

It wasn't so easy to clean up the mess. Kipluck kept attacking me while I was trying to hold my breath and scrape the rug clean with wet paper towels. When I shrugged him off my back, he went for my shoes. When I kicked him away from my feet, he dived for a towel. When I snatched that from him, he tugged on my shirt.

I gathered up the stinky towels, tried to stand up, and heard my shirt rip. I had to get down and unhook his little curved fangs before I could get to the kitchen garbage can. Dad was cooking breakfast. "Doesn't smell too good in here," he said.

I hated putting Kipluck in the goat shed before I left

for the school bus. I had to do it, though. Until Dad attached wire screening to the wooden fence around our property, Kipluck would be able to crawl out of the yard. If he got killed running in the road, that would be worse than locking him in the goat shed.

Jo Mae got on the bus two stops beyond mine. She looked around nervously for a seat while she came down the aisle. "Jo Mae. Jo Mae. Here!" After she saw my waving arms, her face relaxed into a smile.

"I didn't think you'd be taking a bus, too," she said as she settled down beside me.

We compared our new addresses and decided we must live about a half mile apart. If we cut through fields, it might be less. She said her new place was just "a little ol' shack." I said mine couldn't be much bigger, but it had a huge yard and I had a puppy!

I spent the rest of the ride telling Jo Mae all the things that Kipluck did and how cute he was and how it was too bad his claw caught in Brittany's lip, but maybe now she wouldn't come back. Jo Mae shook her head doubtfully. "I don't know. If her mama wants your daddy . . ."

Jack was hanging around the schoolyard when our bus pulled in. I hopped down the bus steps, rushed up, and grabbed his shoulder. "I got my wolf puppy. I got him from Mrs. Thompson. He's mostly white, but his back is grayish and he's got a gray mask."

"Awright!" Jack said. "Do you have a strong fence?"

"Not yet," I told him. "We're going to put one up. Mrs. Thompson said to bury the wire in a four-inch trench and then pour in concrete mix. When it rains, she said, the mix will harden and Kipluck won't be able to dig out."

"That's what my uncle did. But you better build it in a hurry. Wolves are used to traveling in a large territory."

The first bell rang. As we all headed for the school building, I worried a bit about how fast my dad would build the fence. He doesn't do much hurrying. My mom used to say she'd never enter him in a slug race because the slugs would beat him.

When Miss Jewell finished taking roll, Mr. Douglas came in the room with a big box. He stood quietly in front of the room for our attention. We gave it to him, of course. We knew if we didn't, Miss Jewell wouldn't let us go out for lunch recess.

I guess Mr. Douglas didn't know that because he complimented her on what a fine class she had. Miss Jewell smiled sweetly.

"I've got the prizes here for the students who have turned in their sponsors' money." He looked down in the box. "Quite a few prizes for this class."

Some of the kids leaned forward in their seats, trying to look in the box, too. I didn't. And Jack didn't.

"Jenifer Sawyer," Mr. Douglas called out.

Jenny came up to him and he gave her a jacket with a heart on the pocket.

"Sharon Hinkler?"

Sharon came up and was given a glow rope.

"Jack Hanson?"

Jack got up slowly. First Mr. Douglas handed him a jacket. Then he gave him a glow rope. Jack tossed that to me. Last, Mr. Douglas gave him a pair of red jogging shorts.

Jack held the shorts in front of him. The legs came down to his knees. He bunched up the top to fit his skinny waist with one hand, waved his other hand in the air, and swiveled his hips like a hula dancer. We all laughed.

Mr. Douglas took the shorts away from him. "How about settling for a T- shirt and another jump rope?"

Jack took the T-shirt and tossed me the second glow rope. I noticed Sharon Hinkler didn't look happy about that. I thought the ropes were neat. One was orange and one was red. They both had wooden handles. The ropes in the gym just had knots tied at the ends.

After Mr. Douglas handed out all the prizes, Miss Jewell started us on our reading. I put my glow ropes in my desk and got down to work. The ache for my mom wasn't hurting so bad these days.

At lunch, Jack turned his chair around to my desk. He reminded me again that I'd have to get a fence up fast. Wolves live in packs. And mine might look for other animals to play with. Jenny brought her chair over. While I was telling both of them about Brittany and the claw, Miss Jewell stopped by my desk.

"You have a wolf hybrid?" she said after she listened to my story awhile. "There's a book in the library called *Kavic the Wolf Dog*. As soon as we're finished with *How to Eat Fried Worms*, I'll get it and read it to the class." She ran her fingers through the ends of my long hair. "And Marianne, I like the way you've been working today."

When Miss Jewell moved on to another group of kids, Jenny told me, "If you keep on working, you can be a Master Wizard before the end of school. Mr. Douglas lets the new group of kids have any job they want for the last two weeks. You could be an office girl with me." She tilted her head towards Jack. "And he could be on the stage crew for the awards assembly during the last week of school, if he ever stopped getting into trouble."

"I'd like to be an office girl," I said.

"I wouldn't mind being on the stage crew," Jack put in.

It suddenly dawned on both Jenny and me that Jack

hadn't been in trouble since his fight with Leon. To avoid our stares, he ducked his head to take a bite of his sandwich. I don't think he wanted us to see the pink that was spreading under the freckles on his face.

I thought the bus ride home would never end. Jo Mae said good-bye to me at her stop. I kept my arm on the seat in front of me, ready to dash off at my stop.

Kipluck started scratching on the door of the goat shed as soon as I hit the backyard. When I let him out, he leaped for me. I put my books on the grass and kneeled down to hug him and he covered my face with his little puppy kisses.

He hopped up the porch steps after me. I got a glass of milk for me and puppy chow for him. After we ate, I took the broom out to the shed to sweep it clean. Straw was stuck all over Kipluck's fur and he smelled like a goat.

The job wouldn't have taken very long if I hadn't had to pry Kipluck's teeth off the broom after every sweep. I finally gave up and went back to the house for the dust mop. The first time I swished it over the floor, he dropped the broom and dashed for the strings on the mop.

The shed was clean, but I was sweating by the time Dad got home. At dinner, I tried to talk to him about getting the fence up fast. He seemed to think Kipluck would be all right in the shed until the weekend. "I'll work on the fence then," he promised.

The next morning, Kipluck struggled to get away from me when I tried to drag him through the shed door. It took me about ten minutes to get him stuffed inside and I was almost late for the bus.

It Won't Help to Cry

The first few days I had Kipluck, he stayed near the house. But gradually he investigated more and more of the yard. He especially liked the dead branches he found under the apple trees. Sometimes I brought my homework outdoors and worked on it while he chewed the wood into splinters.

Reading didn't seem so boring when I had Kipluck beside me. After I moved up to the gold cards in the SRA kit, Miss Jewell was pleased. She said I might even get to be a Master Wizard if I made it to the brown cards in the next two weeks.

On Thursday afternoon, I left Kipluck while I ran

into the house to answer the phone. It was Dad making his afternoon call to see if I was all right. When I came back outside, I couldn't find Kipluck. I searched all around the yard. I couldn't figure out how he disappeared so fast. I finally found him three houses down, playing with a black dog on the side of the road.

As soon as I got up to him, he turned from the dog with a big smile on his face. "No, no!" I scolded. "You have to stay in your yard. It's dangerous out here."

From the way his tail drooped, I was sure he understood that he'd done something bad. I wasn't sure he understood what, though. That night when I put him to bed on the porch I felt uneasy. Jack's warnings made me nervous. My dad said not to worry. Dogs know where their meals come from. I didn't argue back that Kipluck wasn't all dog.

I opened the kitchen door in the morning, expecting to find him all waggy-tailed and eager for loves and breakfast. He wasn't there. I called him. He didn't come.

I went around to the front of the house and called some more. There he came down the road with his tongue hanging out of his mouth. When he jumped up on me in a happy greeting, I decided it was useless to scold him again. I wished and I wished I could do something about getting the fence up faster, though.

After school that day, Kipluck crawled all over me

when I opened the door of the shed. But when I went inside to get his empty water bowl, he backed away into the yard. "No, no," I told him, "I'm not going to put you in again now."

He hated that shed. And I hated worrying about him running away. I thought maybe if I started the trench, my dad might help me in the evening. When he promised he'd "work on the fence" during the weekend, that didn't mean he'd finish it. I dragged the shovel out of the garage.

Fortunately, Kipluck couldn't bite into metal. He chewed on his nylon bone while I dug into the dirt. I hadn't gotten very far when Lacy drove up next door.

She walked over to pet Kipluck and tell me my shovel looked pretty big. "I know," I said. "It's my dad's."

"I think I've got one with a shorter handle. After I get out of my work clothes, I'll bring it over."

Her "work clothes" were a blue suit with a lavender blouse. Her long hair was braided around her head and she carried a black leather briefcase. I wondered if she was a lawyer or an insurance saleswoman. When she came back, she was wearing jeans. One long pigtail flopped down her back. I got up the nerve to ask her what she did.

"I'm a social worker," she said. "I find foster homes for children who are neglected or hurt."

I put down the big shovel and took the one she gave me. "That must be a sad job."

She nodded. "It is, sometimes. But some other times, when the foster parents are kind and I know the children are safe, it can be a happy job."

I guessed so. But it was bad enough losing my mom. I'd hate to be taken away from my dad. Even if he were ever mean to me.

Lacy went off to ride her horse. I hacked away at the ground until Dad came home. He gave me a hug and let Kipluck tug at his newspaper instead of his pants leg. "Where'd you get the shovel?" he asked.

"Lacy lent it to me."

He raised his shoulders and stared up at the sky. "I guess I'll just be forced to return it to her after dinner."

I was too worried about getting the fence done to think that was funny. "Couldn't we work on the trench a little while first?"

"We-ell, maybe until the ball game comes on."

I let out a big sigh. Of all the things to keep from our old house, it had to be the rickety card table and the stupid TV. Dad ruffled my hair. "After I change my clothes, I'll get something nice out of the back of the station wagon."

I hoped it would be the wire fencing. It wasn't. It was two recliner chairs. I had to admit they were neat.

You can stretch way back in them with your feet on a footrest or you can sit up straight. We sat up straight to eat our TV dinners.

Afterwards, Dad worked on the trench with me. I didn't say so, but I was glad to quit when he did. He carried the shovel back to Lacy and I went in the house to put Band-Aids on my blisters.

Much to my relief, Kipluck came hopping up the steps as soon as I called him in the morning. He thought Saturday and Sunday were great. He wasn't put in the shed and he got to tag after Dad and me all day.

By Sunday evening, the trench was dug. Dad said he'd buy the wire fencing during the week and we'd get it up the next Saturday. I was disappointed, but I couldn't think of any way to make him go faster.

Before I went to bed, I took Kipluck to his blanket on the porch. "You stay there now," I told him. He put his head on his paws and looked up at me with his almond eyes. I gave him an extra love before I went in the house.

He wasn't on the porch in the morning. He didn't come when I called. I walked around to the front of the house and called some more. I was feeling impatient because he might make me miss the bus.

I called and called. He still didn't come. My impatience was turning into panic. I ran down the road a ways, calling and calling. But no Kipluck came clippety-clip into sight.

I went back to the house and looked under the porch where I thought he might be sleeping. He liked to crawl under things and into small places. I searched around the shed and in the garage.

Instead of telling Dad where I was going, I raced into the street again, ran up and around the houses. Lacy had already left for work, but I looked in her barn and under her porch. I couldn't find Kipluck anywhere. I went to the fields behind the houses, calling and calling, my heart pounding with fear.

When I got back to the road, some kids were walking down to the bus stop. "Have any of you seen a white and gray puppy?" I asked them.

They hadn't.

I asked a man who was climbing in his car. "No," he said, "I'm sorry. I haven't."

I raced to my house. Dad was just coming out the front door. "Where've you been?" He was scowling with annoyance. He was probably late for work.

"Kipluck's gone," I told him. "I can't find him any-where."

"Well, it won't help to cry. He can't have gone far. Go get your jacket and we'll hunt for him on the way to school."

"But what if we don't see him?" I wiped my tears away with my arm.

"He'll come back. Even puppies can find their way home. Now, go get your jacket or we won't have time to search."

I ran in the house for my jacket. Dad already had the car started up when I climbed in. I'd forgotten my arithmetic book, but I didn't care.

"Which way have you gone?" he asked.

I pointed down the road past Lacy's house. "That way."

"All right." He turned the steering wheel. "We'll go the other way."

Dad drove slowly along the streets. I had my head out the window, calling and calling and calling. But there was no white and gray puppy. There was no puppy anywhere. As Dad circled the car around to the grade school, I was crying again. "I don't want to go to school. I'll wait for him at home."

"No, you won't. You go on in to class. Kipluck will probably be there when you get back to the house. Don't worry about it."

"That isn't any help," I said.

"I haven't got more help right now. I've got to get to work." He leaned over to kiss me good-bye. "I'll phone Animal Control when I get to the office."

I shrank back from him. "The dog pound! They'll kill him."

"No, they wait three days before they put an animal to sleep. We won't leave him there one day."

I stumbled out of the car. I could barely see through my tears. Jo Mae was the first kid I bumped into. "How come you weren't on the bus . . ." she started out. "Ohhh, what's the matter?"

"My puppy ran away," I told her.

"Ohhh, no." She put her arm around me and walked me to my room.

Before Jack slid into his seat, he stared at me. "What happened to you?"

"Kipluck's gone."

"When?"

"This morning before I could lock him in the goat shed."

Jack shook his head. "You should have got your fence up."

Jenny came over to my desk and I had to tell her, too.

"What's going on?" Miss Jewell asked when she saw us all crowded together.

"Marianne lost her wolf-dog," Jack told her.

Miss Jewell closed her eyes a second, muttered, "Oh, my—" She stopped herself, and said, "I'm sorry, Marianne."

Instead of starting us on our reading after she took roll, Miss Jewel read some more of *How to Eat Fried Worms*. The rest of the kids laughed at the funny places. I just stared at the blackboard, hating my whole life. If my mom were alive, she would have made my dad finish the fence.

At recess, Jack tried to make me feel better by telling me that sometimes wolf hybrids go out to hunt. I thought Kipluck was too little to hunt, but I hoped anyway. I hoped and hoped on the bus riding home and Jo Mae hoped with me.

I raced from the bus stop to my house, praying I'd see my white and gray puppy on the porch waiting for me. He wasn't there. He wasn't in the front yard or in the backyard. He wasn't anywhere.

You're All I've Got

After tramping up and down the road, asking at every door if someone had seen a puppy, I came back to sit on my porch. I was so tired and sad I just sat there seeing pictures of Kipluck in my mind. Kipluck with his head on his paws watching me leave to go to bed. Kipluck rolling over to have his fat tummy scratched. And the one that made me saddest of all, little Kipluck backing away from the shed he hated.

Lacy drove up to her house. I caught up with her on the way to her front door. "Did you happen to see Kipluck anywhere?"

"No, why? Is he gone?"

"He ran away this morning." After I said this, I felt my face scrunch up and tears run down my cheeks.

"Oh, honey, that's too bad." She put her arm around me. "Come on in. I'll put on my boots and we'll ride Zimba out to look for him."

"I've looked and looked and my dad's looked with the car," I told her.

"Yes, but Zimba can go where cars can't go."

Zimba is a great big cream-colored horse with a black mane and black tail. He flicked his ears and arched his neck around to peek at me. I didn't know how I'd ever get on him.

Lacy did. She brought a box out of the barn and placed it next to him on the grass. "Now stand up on that," she told me. "Put your left foot in the stirrup. Swing your right leg over his back. I'll give you a push up and you take your foot out of the stirrup and grab onto his mane."

It worked. I sat way up there while Lacy took the box away, put her foot in the stirrup, and swung up to sit behind me. She reached around to take the reins from Zimba's neck, clacked her tongue, and we were off.

First, we rode all through the fields behind our houses. Then we went up the hill and into some woods. I called and called. Once I saw something white behind some bushes, but it was only a sack with empty pop bottles in it.

The afternoon sun was hot on our backs when we came down out of the woods. Lacy trotted Zimba up and down side roads. I called and called Kipluck until my voice was just a scratchy whisper.

"He must have followed a dog home and is playing in someone's backyard," Lacy said. "You probably should get him a female to keep him company while you're in school."

I probably should, but I didn't think my dad would go for it. I thought he'd want a davenport first. And all I really wanted was Kipluck.

Lacy turned Zimba towards her house. It was the end of searching for that afternoon. I tried hard not to start crying again as Zimba cantered up to the barn like a big rocking horse.

After Lacy helped me down, she asked, "What happened to your mother?"

"She died. She was coming back from visiting my grandpa and the airplane crashed."

"Was that the jet that crashed outside of Denver?"

"Yes," I said.

She pulled the saddle off Zimba's back. "I remember seeing that on TV. It must have been very rough for you."

I nodded.

"Would you like to come in for some tea? I made a coconut cake yesterday."

"No thank you," I said. "Thanks for helping me look for Kipluck, though."

I went on back to my house while Lacy took the saddle into the barn. Most times coconut cake would have sounded good, but not this day. I sat by myself in one of the recliner chairs until the big, empty room got so depressing it drove me outside.

I wandered around the porch. My legs felt like roasted chicken legs from being spread out over Zimba's back. The fragrance of the roses made me sick. I picked one bud anyway, sat down on the steps, and leaned my head against the railing. I sat there until Dad got home, not even bothering to wipe away the tears dripping down my chin.

Dad was carrying a sack. He placed it between his legs as he sat down beside me. "Your mother used to like roses."

"I know." I began tearing each petal off the bud and dropping it on the steps.

He watched me for a minute. "I have a little good news. I went to the Animal Control center. Kipluck wasn't there, but they said they hadn't had any calls about a puppy being hit by a car."

I leaned my head over my lap and sobbed. The thought of Kipluck dead on the road hurt so bad I couldn't stand it.

Dad pulled me over to him. "I brought home some marking pens and cardboard so we could make lost-puppy signs. We'll put them on the telephone poles in the neighborhood. OK? We'll write our phone number on them and offer a ten-dollar reward. That should get kids looking out for him.

"Come on. Let's eat something and then go make the signs, OK?"

We made ten signs. Stuck them all up and down the road. I called and called some more, but my voice was almost gone.

In bed, the picture of Kipluck with his nose on his paws kept floating in my head. He was watching me with his slanted eyes. They had turned almost yellow before he ran away.

I tried to think of something else. Something besides my mom. Something to rock my mind to sleep. I couldn't think of anything.

"Do your work anyway," Jack told me at school the next morning. "So you can be a Master Wizard. My uncle said his wolf-dog was gone for two days before he fenced him in."

I did my work. I didn't care one way or the other. Miss Jewell gave my head a pat as she walked by.

On the bus ride home, Jo Mae kept trying to make me feel better. "That puppy's going to come home," she insisted. "Sometimes I just know things. Grandma says I'm like her. I can feel things in my bones."

Watching Jo Mae get off the bus, I thought she was a really neat person. Some kids, like Sharon, were mean to her and some kids didn't pay much attention to her because she was poor and different. But I liked her.

I didn't want to get my hopes up, though. After I got off the bus, I tried to walk slowly. But the nearer I came to my house, the faster my legs went. As I passed Lacy's, I thought I saw something white on my porch.

I raced to my gate and pushed it open. There he was, flashing down the steps. I crouched to the ground as he leaped on me and covered my chin with his wet puppy kisses.

"Where have you been, Kipluck? Where have you been?" I took his soft, furry head in my hands and looked into his eyes. "Where did you go?"

His only answer was more kisses. I hugged him to me and cried, "I haven't got a mother, Kipluck. My mom died. You can't do this to me again. You can't run away, Kipluck. You're all I've got. You and Dad are all I've got. If you aren't here when I come home, I'm all alone."

Kipluck pulled away from me and sat with his head held stiffly back. He didn't seem to understand my cries and tears. I tugged his head close to mine. "You can't run away ever again, Kipluck. You can't leave me, please."

I petted his fur over and over until I remembered. "Oh, are you hungry?" I asked him. I gathered my books up from the grass and he followed me into the house.

Mostly he wanted water. After that, he gulped down a can and a half of dog food. I was thinking to myself that I would keep him in the house at night until the fence was finished. He could sleep with me. So I'd know exactly where he was.

We were playing in the yard when Lacy drove up in front of her house. I called to her, "Kipluck's home! Kipluck came home."

She came right over. "It looks like you've been crying, honey," she said.

I ducked my head down. "Yes. I was so glad to see him. And I don't want him to run away again."

"I bet you don't." She tucked her skirt under her and sat down on the step beside me. "You got lonesome, huh?"

"Don't you get lonesome in your house alone?"

"Sometimes," she agreed. "Sometimes in the evening."

"You never got married?"

"Once I was. But it turned out that he wasn't a very kind man."

"And you didn't have any children?"

"No, I never had any children," she said. "And it was lucky I didn't, because my husband wouldn't have made a very nice father."

"My father's nice. Except he's slow."

Lacy smiled. "I noticed. But I think you have to look around at other kids' dads and see they have faults, too. There are worse things than being slow. You can love your dad even if he isn't perfect."

"Oh, I do. It's just that I lost Kipluck."

"And that was hard." She looked into my face. "Especially after you lost your mother."

I nodded. Talking to Lacy was like talking to a friend. I wasn't even embarrassed when I asked her questions. "Didn't you ever wish you could have children?" I wondered.

"Yes. I still wish it."

"Why don't you take home one of those kids who has bad parents?" This time I looked in her face to see what she would answer.

"Lots of times I've wanted to take one in," she said. "But it's against the rules of my job."

My dad drove up then. There were big rolls of wire

fencing sticking out of the back of his station wagon. "Good," I said. "I told him Kipluck was back when he called. He promised he'd bring the wire and concrete tonight."

After Dad gave me a kiss and greeted Lacy, I asked, "You got everything?"

"Not quite. The concrete was too heavy to carry in one load. I'll bring the rest on Friday." Kipluck was jumping on him, trying to say hello. Dad petted him and rolled him around the grass.

"How about going out to dinner to celebrate?" It seemed like he meant both Lacy and me.

"Oh, I don't want to put Kipluck in the shed now," I protested. "Couldn't we get some Chinese food to go and have a picnic?"

"Sure."

"And Lacy, too?"

"Sure." Dad smiled.

"Let's have it on the picnic table in my backyard," Lacy suggested. "And I'll make some iced tea."

Dad looked up from playing with Kipluck. "Sure," he said again, and his smile was even bigger.

I got tired right after we ate. I hadn't had much sleep the last two nights. "You look done in," Dad said.

"Why don't you take Kipluck to our house and I'll help Lacy clean up."

"All right." I got slowly up from the picnic bench. "And he'll have to stay inside tonight so he doesn't run away again."

Before Dad could object, Lacy put in quickly, "My dog always slept with me when I was a kid."

By the time I had had my bath and was settled in bed with Kipluck, Dad still wasn't home. That was OK with me. And the rule that Lacy couldn't take in kids from her job was OK with me, too.

The Thief

At school everybody was glad that Kipluck had come back. Jo Mae said, "I knew it. I could just feel him coming home." Jenny jumped up and down. Diane said, "Rad!" Miss Jewell said, "Thank goodness." And Jack said, "Awright! Now get your fence up."

We did. My dad started out early Saturday morning. He pushed the first big roll of wire against the wooden posts beside the gate. I followed after him with a wheelbarrow that held concrete mix and a shovel. After Dad nailed the wire to a post, he shoveled concrete along the trench.

We were at the corner next to Lacy's house, when

she came out her door. Her yellow hair was hanging down her back, the way I liked it best. She watched us a minute and then crawled through the boards of the old wooden fence into our yard. "Looks like you could use a little help."

She unwound the big roll of wire ahead of Dad so all he had to do was nail and shovel. It went faster this way. I was beat by eleven o'clock when Dad suggested we stop to make some sandwiches and coffee.

After he and Lacy went in the kitchen, I stretched out on the grass. I didn't get to relax very long, though, because Kipluck woke up from his nap and leaped on me. "You crazy dog," I told him and rolled on top of him. He squirmed out from under me, crouched down like his daddy did, and then made another leap for me.

"Soup's on!" Dad yelled from the kitchen. I raced Kipluck to the house. He ate puppy chow while I ate tuna-fish sandwiches at the card table with Dad and Lacy. Every so often I had to stop eating to scratch.

"Mosquito bites?" Lacy asked.

"No, flea bites," I told her. "Kipluck's been sleeping with me."

"Marianne!" Dad said.

"Well, he must have gotten the fleas when he ran away. If I'd told you," I explained, "you'd have made Kipluck stay on the porch and then he'd run away again."

"You're wrong," he corrected me. "I would have squirted you both with flea spray."

"Anyway, as soon as the fence is done, Kipluck can sleep outside."

"Wolves are social animals," Lacy said. "What you need is a female to keep him company. Then you could have puppies, too."

Puppies! I'd love a whole batch of puppies.

Dad carefully placed his cup on the wobbly table. "What we need first," he said, "is some dining room furniture."

"Maybe we could get a female in the fall," I suggested.

Lacy shook her head. "Wolves only have cubs in the spring. I should think wolf hybrids would be the same." She looked at me thoughtfully. "When's your birthday?"

"July ninth." I put down the crust of my sandwich and scratched my wrist where I had three flea bites in a row.

Dad leaned across the table. "How about another cup of coffee, Lacy?"

"Hmm, I think not," Lacy said, standing up. "I think Marianne needs that fence up more than I need coffee."

I loved that Lacy!

We were way in the backyard by the apple trees

when Jo Mae showed up. She had found the way through the fields to our house all by herself. "See?" She ducked her head shyly and held her hand out to me. "My Grandma gave me this ring. She wore it when she was a girl."

The stone was the same color as Jo Mae's eyes, a pretty light blue. Lacy admired the ring, too.

I explained to Jo Mae that I would have to work for a while. She offered to help, but there was really nothing for her to do. "Play with Kipluck," I said. That suited her fine because she just loved "that little ol' puppy." They ran around the trees after each other while I pushed the wheelbarrow along the trench. Kipluck had the big smile on his face that he gets whenever he's having a great time.

Dad gave a last big pound of the hammer on a corner post. There was one side of the yard left to go. It was only two o'clock, but I was afraid he was going to quit. "You through for the day?" I asked, really disappointed. Since he knew about the fleas, I was sure he wouldn't let Kipluck in my bed that night.

"Nope, have to do a store run. No more nails." He raised his eyebrows at me. "And while I'm out, I'll get some flea spray."

I shrank away from him, but Lacy put her arm around me. "Don't worry, honey," she said. "He'll spray Kipluck and you can take a shower."

106

After Dad and Lacy left for the store, Jo Mae and I threw a Frisbee back and forth. Once in a while, we'd miss a catch and Kipluck would pounce on the Frisbee. We were chasing Kipluck around the yard, trying to get it back from him, when Brittany and Mrs. James drove up.

I explained to them that Dad wasn't home.

Mrs. James's black hair was done up in stiff curls all over her head. She patted them with her hand. "Well, when will he return, dear?"

I hated it when she called me "dear." When Lacy called me "honey," it made me warm inside. "I'm not sure when he'll be back," I said.

Jo Mae had gotten the Frisbee away from Kipluck by then, so I introduced her to Mrs. James and Brittany. Kipluck kept jumping up on Jo Mae, trying to get at the Frisbee.

"You'd better be careful of that dog," Brittany warned her. "He'll hurt you."

"No he won't!" I usually try not to cause trouble, but that made me mad. "And I might be getting a female to keep him company."

Mrs. James's jaw pushed forward. "One of those animals is bad enough. You don't need two."

"He split my lip open," Brittany said. "I suppose you think that didn't hurt?"

Jo Mae was hanging back behind me. I pulled her

forward by her hand. "Look at Jo Mae's new ring. Her grandma gave it to her."

Brittany bent over Jo Mae's outstretched finger. "What kind of a stone is that?"

Mrs. James took a close look. "An aquamarine, isn't it?"

Jo Mae nodded. "My grandma wore it when she was a girl."

"I wish I had a ring." Brittany shot her mother a nasty glance. "Everybody else has one."

Mrs. James ignored Brittany and shifted her attention to me. "As long as we're here, why don't all you girls play Frisbee? I'll wait in the car for a while."

I knew I should take Mrs. James in the house and let her sit on one of the recliner chairs, but I was afraid she'd stay there until Lacy and Dad got back. Then Lacy might leave. I moved out in the grass. Jo Mae tossed me the Frisbee and I tossed it to Brittany.

Every time Brittany caught it, she threw it fast so Kipluck would gallop away from her. I thought Mrs. James would never get tired waiting, but she finally did. She honked the horn twice.

"Just a minute," Brittany called to her. "I have to go to the bathroom."

Brittany went into the house. Jo Mae and I flopped down on the ground. We let Kipluck have the Frisbee so he wouldn't attack us. After a while, he got tired of chewing on it and jumped on us anyway.

"That girl's been in there a long time," Jo Mae whispered to me. "Wonder what she's doing?"

I wondered, too. Just as I got to the porch, Brittany walked out the front door.

"Did you need something?" I asked.

"No," Brittany said, hurrying past me.

Almost as soon as she and Mrs. James left, Dad and Lacy came home. I mentioned casually that Brittany and her mother had been visiting. Dad gave me a quick look, but he didn't say anything.

Jo Mae had to leave at four o'clock. At five o'clock Dad stopped pounding, dangled the hammer from his hand, and rubbed his shoulder. "How about we knock this off and all go out to dinner?"

"Oh, come on," Lacy said impatiently. "There's only one section left. Let's finish it up."

He finished it up, much to my relief. But I worried a bit about Lacy. I didn't know whether she liked my dad or not.

They seemed to get along all right at dinner. We went to a Mexican restaurant that Lacy knew about. I wished we'd gone to the Chinese place so I could eat fried prawns.

When we got home, Kipluck bounced against the gate

as soon as he saw me get out of the car. He was a little disappointed, though, when he had to go to sleep on the porch.

Before climbing into bed, I pulled back the covers to search for fleas. I wondered if I should spray inside my sheets. But if I did, then wouldn't the fleas jump on me?

I was almost asleep, when the memory of Brittany walking out of our house came up in my mind. She had kept her left hand in her jeans pocket as she hurried past me. The ring! I hopped out of bed, opened my bottom dresser drawer, took out my mom's jewel box, and looked inside. I didn't see the garnet ring. I searched all through the earrings and beads. My mother's ring wasn't there.

How Stupid Can You Get?

At breakfast, I told my dad about Mom's ring being gone. I explained how Brittany had wanted a ring and how she'd stayed in the house by herself for a long time. Dad thoughtfully sipped his hot coffee. "We can't be sure she took it, but I guess we'd better go see."

The cooked-cabbage smell was still in the halls of the old apartment house. I stood behind Dad while he knocked on the James's door. Mrs. James answered his knock.

"What a nice surprise. Come in. Come in." She gave us her big, white smile.

Brittany was in the living room, reading the Sunday

funnies. When she saw us, she stuck her left hand in her jeans pocket, stood up, and took a step towards the hall door.

"We have something we'd like to talk to you about," Dad said as he and Mrs. James settled into the fuzzy peach chairs.

"You sound serious," Mrs. James said.

"I guess I am." He nodded at Brittany who was edging out of the room. "Won't you sit back down, Brittany. This concerns you, too."

"Well, I was just going to wash my hands. We had pig sausages for breakfast."

"Sit down," Mrs. James ordered.

Brittany sat on the corner of the davenport with me.

"If you don't mind," Dad told Mrs. James, "I'd like to make a request of Brittany."

"Fine with me," Mrs. James said.

He turned to Brittany. "Will you please take your hand out of your pocket?"

She slowly pulled her hand free. The garnet ring hung over the knuckle on her finger.

"May I have that?" Dad asked. "That was Marianne's mother's ring."

Mrs. James rose to her feet, went over to Brittany, and took the ring away from her. Before she handed it to Dad, she examined it closely. "Jim, is this real gold?"

"Yes, it is," he said.

"Oh, my, I thought it was costume jewelry. Marianne should never have given it to Brittany."

"I didn't," I said. "Brittany went into our house by herself when she told you she was going to the bathroom. And stayed a long time."

"You followed me in the house and gave me the ring." Brittany stared into my eyes with that mean look on her face.

"No I didn't." I stared straight back at her. "I met you on the porch and you went right by me."

Red color covered Mrs. James's forehead and poured down to her neck. She had to remember Brittany going into our house alone and coming out our door alone. She could see us from her car. "I can't believe this." Mrs. James clasped her hands to her chest. "I don't know what to say."

"Maybe Brittany has something to say," Dad suggested.

Brittany darted one frightened look at her mom and then concentrated on the toes of her slippers.

"Well," Dad said, standing up. "I'm sorry this happened, but I'm glad to have the ring back."

I almost tripped over my shoes going out the door. When Dad closed it, I bent down to tie the laces on my Keds. We could hear Mrs. James's voice coming through the wall. It didn't sound the same as when she'd apologized to us over and over.

"You idiot!" she raged. "Why did you do such a dumb thing? How stupid can you get? Now how are we ever going to see them again?"

Who cares, I thought to myself.

On the way to our car, Dad didn't say anything about what we'd heard. Instead, he suggested that we check out davenports on the way home.

We checked out about twenty of them. Most of them were fat with icky colors. There was a neat, navy-blue leather one, but it cost two thousand dollars.

"Lacy has lots of furniture," I told Dad as we left the last store. "She could move in with us and rent her house."

"Oh, what about her horse?"

"Well, she doesn't have to rent her barn," I explained. "Just her house."

Dad looked down at me with his eyebrows raised. "You'd like that, huh?"

Sure I would. Who wouldn't?

Lacy was working in her yard, when we got home. "I'm starved," I whispered to Dad. "Let's invite Lacy out to dinner."

Lacy is the kind of person who doesn't make a big fuss about being fancy. "I'd like to go," she told us, "if you don't mind my jeans."

"That's what we're wearing," Dad said.

"Nobody dresses up at the Chinese restaurant," I reminded them. They agreed, so I got my fried prawns.

After the waiter cleared the table, he left a fresh pot of tea and a plate with three fortune cookies. I chose the first one, broke it open, and took out the slip of paper.

"What does it say, honey?" Lacy asked.

"It says, 'You will get your wish.' "

"Don't tell what it is," she warned me, "or it won't come true."

While I watched her break open the next cookie, I tried to decide on a wish. I wanted another puppy so Kipluck wouldn't be lonesome while I was in school. I couldn't have my mom back, of course, but I thought Lacy might make a nice mother.

" 'Good news coming,' " Lacy announced. "I hope it's a raise."

Dad straightened out his paper. " 'You will get a lot done in this world.' "

"Slowly," I added, and they both laughed.

After we left the restaurant, Dad dropped me off at our house so he and Lacy could go for a ride in the warm, spring evening. I played with Kipluck awhile and then went to bed. I woke up a bit later to the sound of rain. Good, I thought, the cement in the trench will get hard.

Then I wondered if Kipluck was wet. He always dragged his blanket around the porch and it might be out beyond the edge of the roof. I got up to see.

He wasn't on the porch. I called, "Kipluck, Kipluck."

He slowly crawled out from under the steps to give me some sleepy licks on my chin. When I heard Dad's car, I stopped petting Kipluck's soft fur, stood up from my crouch, and listened for voices. They weren't coming nearer. They were fading away.

I went around to the side of our porch. Dad and Lacy were going up Lacy's steps. When they were right under her front door light, I saw Lacy turn to Dad, reach up her arms, and pull his head down to hers. Awright! Lacy did like my dad! I gave Kipluck a good-night hug and tiptoed back to bed.

Master Wizards

Monday morning, Jenny caught up with me on the way to our classroom. "Listen, I know something neat." She pulled me over against the wall. "But don't tell anyone, because I'm not supposed to tell you. You and Jack and Lester are going to be Master Wizards!"

"Really! How do you know?"

"Shh!" Jenny didn't say any more until Sharon had gone by. "I know because I worked in the office Friday morning. The secretary had me take the certificates to the bus drivers and the playground teachers to get them signed. We're going to have a Master Wizard meeting today and you guys are going to be invited."

"You mean Mrs. Wilson signed Jack's certificate?"

"Yes, she did, and she wrote a note to Mr. Douglas saying Jack had been a little gentleman on the playground for the last month." Jenny put her hand over her mouth to cover her giggles.

We giggled all the way to our room. Jack was leaning on the other side of my desk when I got to it.

"Hey, look at the red bird out there." He pointed to the windows.

"Where?" I couldn't see any red bird.

"I guess you missed it," he said.

I sat down in my chair.

Ppppuuttt!!!

I sprang up again.

"Marianne!" Jack shouted. "Shame on you!"

Everybody in the classroom was laughing. I yanked the whoopee cushion off my seat. "Jack, you jerk!"

I was going to throw the cushion in the waste basket, but he jumped over my seat and grabbed it. We were both tugging on it, when Diane said, "Cool it. Here comes Miss Jewell."

I let go of the cushion and Jack stuffed it in his desk before Miss Jewell got in the room.

During reading, I was trying to figure out how to warn Jack about the Master Wizard meeting. It wasn't a very big honor to get a certificate and pin so late in the year. Still, I didn't want him to miss being on the stage crew for the awards assembly.

I felt Miss Jewell watching me. I got down to work answering the questions on my brown card. I knew it was because I'd made it to the brown cards that she'd put me on the Master Wizard list.

We were finished with our reading and working on the Lewis and Clark expedition when Mr. Douglas came to our door. Miss Jewell went out in the hall to talk with him. As soon as she was out of sight, Jack pulled out his whoopee cushion. Before I could get him to listen to me, he was up at Miss Jewell's desk, slipping the cushion under the pad on her chair.

I glanced over at Sharon. She was watching Jack closely. She had that goody-good, tattletale look on her face. I got up and stood in the aisle. "Put that thing back in your desk."

"No way," he said. "And you'd better sit down or you'll get in trouble."

I didn't sit down. I marched up to Miss Jewell's chair, snatched the cushion from under the pad, and threw it in the wastebasket.

"Hey, cut that—"

"Cool it," Tara warned.

Jack slipped into his seat and I hurried toward mine, too late.

"Marianne, what are you doing?" Miss Jewell's smile had turned into a scowl.

"I just put something in the wastebasket."

"You aren't supposed to be away from your desk when I leave the room."

"I'm sorry," I mumbled.

"Well, you really know better." As she walked to the front of the room, she frowned at the piece of paper in her hand. I supposed she was thinking about whether I should be a Master Wizard or not. She tapped the paper several times on the edge of the front table before she made her announcement. "There will be a Master Wizard meeting in the library at ten-fifteen. Jack, Lester, and Marianne have been invited to attend."

Jack raised his hand. "I thought they held those meetings on Friday."

"Mr. Douglas usually does," Miss Jewell agreed. "But he was out of the building last week."

So that's why Jack had the whoopee cushion! After Friday was over, he must have given up on being a Master Wizard.

Miss Jewell nodded at me. "And you'd better get to work, young lady."

I dived into my notebook and wrote furiously on Captain Cook's sighting of majestic Mount Hood. At ten-fifteen, Miss Jewell said the Master Wizards could go to the library. I guessed she was calling Jack and Lester and me Master Wizards, too.

There were about fifty kids in the library. Jack, Lester, Tara, Jenny, and I sat at a table together. Mr. Douglas stood by the card catalog and gave us a talk about how he was always proud to welcome new Master Wizards into the group. He said it didn't matter how long it took to reach a goal. The important thing was to accomplish it.

There were seven new Master Wizards. He called us up to stand beside him. He shook our hands and gave each of us a certificate and pin. And then he started clapping and the rest of the kids clapped for us, too.

When Mr. Douglas asked us what we wanted to do for the school, Mrs. Leland, the librarian, wrote down our jobs. A couple of kids wanted to work in the library. I said I wanted to be an office girl. Jack and Lester said they'd be on the stage crew.

A bowl of punch and a tray of donuts were on the check-out counter. Mrs. Leland told us the new Master Wizards got to be first in line. After we'd carried our food to the table, I asked Jack if he was still mad at me for throwing away his whoopee cushion.

"Naw," he said. "I'll get it back at lunch."

"You'd better take it home then."

"Maybe." He gave me his wicked grin. "Or maybe

I'll put it in my desk until the awards assembly is over."

Jenny poked me. "How's your pup?"

"Great. Except he chewed the handles off one of my glow ropes. And you know what?" I put down my cup of punch and leaned closer to her. "My dad's going out with the lady next door."

Jenny finished the last bite of her donut and wiped her hands on her paper napkin. "So you might get a stepmother."

A fifth grade kid sitting in front of us turned around. "You poor thing," he said.

"What would you call her?" Jenny wondered.

"Lacy, I guess. That's what I call her now."

"What does she call you?" the fifth grade kid asked me.

I couldn't keep a smile from curling around my mouth. "She calls me 'honey,' " I said.

The SLOPPY COPY SlipUP

DyAnne DiSalvo

Holiday House / New York

Acknowledgments:
I would like to thank Ms. Roxanne Adonolfi and the faculty and students
from Joyce Kilmer Elementary School and Stockton Elementary School;
Ms. Harriet Fromme; my son, John Ryan; Adrianne Kalfopoulou; the band
Smash Palace; and my husband, Stephen Butler, for all their exuberant
support and outstanding inspiration.

Printed and Bound in October 2016 at Maple Press, York, PA, USA.
www.holidayhouse.com

13 15 17 19 20 18 16 14 12

Library of Congress Cataloging-in-Publication Data

DiSalvo, DyAnne.
The sloppy copy slipup / by DyAnne DiSalvo.—1st ed.
p. cm.
Summary: Fourth-grader Brian Higman worries about how his teacher Miss
Fromme—nicknamed The General—will react when he fails to hand in a writing
assignment, but he ends up being able to tell his story, after all.
ISBN 0-8234-1947-9
[1. Storytelling—Fiction.   2. Authorship—Fiction.   3. Schools—Fiction.
4. Humorous stories.]   I. Title.

PZ7.D6224Slo 2005
[Fic]—dc22
2004060777

ISBN-13: 978-0-8234-1947-0 (hardcover)
ISBN-13: 978-0-8234-2189-3 (paperback)

For my charming
and lovely nieces,
Madeleine and Rachel

BIG HIG'S DISASTROUS NEWSLETTER

as keyboarded on my computer by Brian Higm

WRITER'S JOURNAL UPDATE

Dear Writer's Journal,
   Today I do not have my homework
and I am about to get another zero.
          Yours truly,
          Guess who?

← my mother

A PERSON WHO CAN MAKE A BIG DEAL OUT OF ANYTHING

Ana is the kind of person who can make a big deal out of anything. Last week when Martin Adaji put a tomato in his fruit painting, Ana made one of her big deals about whether a tomato was a fruit or a vegetable. I was glad when Mrs. Chila said that a tomato could be considered as both. It was a fruit that was used as a vegetable. In the plant group it was actually considered to be a berry.

← TOMATO

BRIAN HIGMAN'S MOTHER FINALLY HITS CEILING!

Really nice kid banished to Siberia for LIFE.
See more inside.

AHHH

TRY THIS NEW RECIPE!

SLOW-ROASTED SURPRISE

Mix one big kid,
one late homework.
Add one angry teacher.
Turn on heat.
Stand back.
Expect anything!

QUOTE OF THE DAY FROM MR. MEYERS AT THE MUSIC STORE:

"Stevie, you send my blood pressure right through the roof."

artwork done by the outstanding Big Hig

WANTED: DEAD OR ALIVE
Brian Higman
Alias Big Hig
REWARD

EXTRA!
Brian Higman sets universal record for most detentions in world history.

BIG HIG'S CLASSROOM WEATHER REPORT:
Will the hurricane hit? Stay tuned for more <u>DISASTROUS</u> <u>NEWS</u>.

BIG HIG HOROSCOPE:
Caution! Planets are crisscrossing. This is NOT your lucky day.

POSITION WANTED:
Experienced person needed to help dig kid out of deep trouble. Send all inquiries to Hig.

This is not a good joke

sorry

OUTSTANDING JOKE:
<u>Question</u>: Why did the centipede cross the road?
<u>Answer:</u> To get to the other side.

SOLVE ALL YOUR PROBLEMS AND WRITE TO MANNERS MATTER:

Dear Manners Matter,
   Do you think it is bad manners for a teacher to fail an unfortunate yet outstanding student without listening to his whole reason first?
           Yours truly,
           A really nice kid

Dear A Really Nice Kid,
   It would be very bad manners, indeed.
           Sincerely,
           Manners Matter

DESPERATE:
Soon-to-be great guitar player seeks bass player who feels the same. Must like rock and roll. <u>SEND PHOTO!</u>

more news coming soon...

contents

Chapter One
An Outstanding Zero

It was Monday morning. The entire kinder-
garten through fifth-grade classes at Franklin
Elementary had just sat down after reciting the
Pledge of Allegiance.

I, Big Hig, was fielding through my backpack, pretending to search for the written assignment I knew I didn't have.

"The word of the day is *outstanding*," my
ex-best friend, Ana Newburg, announced over
the loudspeaker. Why is Ana my ex-best friend?
That's a whole other story I'll get to later.

"O-u-t-s-t-a-n-d-i-n-g." Ana spelled the word
slowly. "It is an adjective meaning exceptional
or terrific. For lunch we will be having *outstanding* macaroni and cheese with *outstanding*
fresh fruit and your choice of *outstanding* juice
or milk. Thank you. Have an *outstanding* day."

Ana held her mouth too close to the microphone and made the loudspeaker screech. "AHHHHH!" Robby Zao fell against his desk and covered his ears. Josh Mendez closed his eyes and made a sour face. I was grateful for any distraction. It was only a matter of time before my teacher, Miss Fromme, began to collect Monday morning's assignment—the first draft— better known to her class as *the sloppy copy*.

After we hand in our sloppy copy it comes back with a mess of corrections and suggestions from Miss Fromme. Like: *Brian, more description for this opening sentence, please.* Or: *Brian, please remember to use your five senses when you write.* Uh! The next rewrite checks for grammar and spelling. *Brian, you do not need all these commas, thank you.* Which finally brings us to the final copy, if we end up living that long.

I personally do not mind writing. The problem is that I never have anything exciting to write about. Thinking up an idea is the hardest part for me. Anything I ever think about writing is either too long, too short, or too boring.

For example, why do the kids call me Big Hig? Simple. I am the biggest kid in our class and my name is Brian Higman. End of story.

2

And how about my family? Well, let's see. I have a mother named Florence. My pop's name is George. My older brother is Denny. My younger brother is Stevie. And I have a dog named Patches.

I guess I could try to write something about them. But that's where the long and boring part comes in.

Once I tried to write about a fishing trip we all went on. It was the day my pop decided we needed to spend some family time together. The sun was shining like pizza. My mother got two fishing poles from the basement and sponged off the cobwebs. Denny and I wrapped five peanut butter and jelly sandwiches in tinfoil. Stevie was in charge of packing the snacks. Pop piled everything, including us, into our Subaru station wagon and off we went. Mom turned up the radio while Denny played an air guitar in the backseat. Stevie counted and re-counted the number of cookies he had in his bag. "One plus two is three. Three plus one is four." I was relieved to know that my little brother did not have any ideas to supply us with any of his so-called entertainment.

When we got to the lake, we unpacked our stuff into the little boat we rented. Well no sooner did Pop finally ripple our canoe to what promised to be a good spot for fishing, when Stevie began to feel sorry for the minnows we were about to use for live bait. He patted his life jacket. "Don't worry, fishies," Stevie said in his superhero voice, "I'll save you." Then he picked up the pail of minnows and emptied the entire bucket into the water, yelling, "Free the fishies! Free the fishies!" You can believe me or not, but this really happened. Who wants to hear a story like that? I didn't think it was very good.

So instead of handing it in to Miss Fromme, I gave her a blank piece of paper. That was the first time I got a red zero.

Miss Fromme says that it is good practice to be aware of the ordinary things that happen in your life and learn to write them down.

Dear Writer's Journal,
    Today I do not have my homework again and I am about to get another zero.
                    Yours truly,
                        guess who?

I was busy thinking of unexciting and ordinary things like journal writing and family fishing trips, when Miss Fromme motioned for the first table to stand. She pressed her lips together in a line. My stomach did a quick flip.

"First table," Miss Fromme said. "Ladies and Gentlemen! Less talk and more attention. This way, please." The kids at the first table made one messy line toward the front of the room. I watched as a pile of written assignments began to stack up on Miss Fromme's desk.

I could tell right away that Miss Fromme was not in a good mood. She did not even say thank you whenever another paper was added to the bunch. "Next table, please," said Miss Fromme.

I swallowed too much air at once and let out a little burp. It was all over for me. One more table and I'd be up there, too.

Ana Newburg walked into the classroom. She was all whoop-de-do from her loudspeaker announcement. She shook her bangs and rushed to her seat where she pulled out her sloppy copy. Ana held it up as if Miss Fromme had already given her an A+.

"Big deal," Robby Zao whispered to her from table three. He chomped on his pencil like a rabbit.

I opened my journal and wrote:

Ana is the kind of person who can make a big deal out of anything. Last week in art class, when Martin Adaji put a tomato in his fruit painting, Ana made one of her big deals about whether a tomato was a fruit or a vegetable. I was glad when Mrs. Chila said that a tomato could be considered as both. It was a fruit that was used as a vegetable. In the plant group it was actually considered to be a berry.

I put my pencil down.

Right now, the last thing I needed was for Ana Newburg to make some kind of big deal about me. After all, I had a very good reason for not having my written assignment. In fact, I had planned to do it all weekend. Only my weekend did not work out as I had planned. Now all I had to do was convince Miss Fromme to give me another chance.

Chapter Two
Don't Mess With the Facts

I sat in my seat and waited for my table to be called. I stared at my blank piece of paper. I could almost imagine the way it would look with the words written neatly on the page. It would have been chock-full of information—just like a newspaper.

The one thing I did know about was newspapers. Besides being the top salesperson at Robins Appliance Store, my pop was also the founder and publisher of *The Franklin Newsletter*.

The Franklin, as it is commonly known in our house, is the town's monthly newsletter. It keeps Franklin neighbors up-to-date on block parties, leaf cleanups, town meetings, horoscopes, weather reports, and other bits of local news that fill up a two-page leaflet. Don't Mess with the Facts is Pop's running motto.

My brother Denny says he's heard Pop recite his motto so many times that he doesn't even hear it anymore. Personally, I think Denny's bad hearing has less to do with my pop's motto and more to do with the so-called entertainment my little brother, Stevie, provides during the course of the day.

"Stevie, you send my blood pressure right through the roof."

I wrote that in my journal, too. That's a direct quote from Mr. Myers who owns the music store in town. And that goes double for me.

"Next table, please," Miss Fromme said. "The rest of the class please open your writers' notebooks and begin to journal your morning."

This is it, I told myself. I stood up. A long, loud bell rang. We were having an *outstanding* fire drill.

"Line leader up front, quickly," Miss Fromme said. "Quickly, quickly. Class, no talking or there will be no recess."

Kala Patel rushed to her position.

Saved by the bell! I love fire drills.

I stepped in line with the rest of my class and followed Kala into the great outdoors. We all went silently down the stairs and out to the back of the school yard.

"How come I never get to be the line leader?" Josh Mendez whispered to me. Josh had both hands stuck inside the pockets of his denim jacket. His glasses were crooked, and he smelled like lemon-scented laundry detergent.

"You were the line leader last month," I whispered back.

"I forgot," said Josh.

"I'm going to report you," Kala warned us.

The last thing I needed was for any more trouble. The autumn day was crisp and breezy. The trees looked like they were waving hello. I blew out a sigh of relief. At least in the school yard, I was temporarily saved. I relaxed a little and began to enjoy it. My mind took a break and started to wander.

Did I happen to mention that I am in the market to buy my first guitar? Well, I am. I've had my eye on a really cool electric guitar that has been in Mr. Myers's music store for about two weeks. It's second-hand, but it's as good as new. Whenever I am in there, which is usually a lot, Mr. Myers lets me check it out.

I always go out of my way never to touch anything or ask Mr. Myers too many questions while I'm in there. Mr. Myers is the nervous type. And my little brother, Stevie, makes him nervous. Mostly I try to go into the music store by myself, but usually I am keeping an eye on Stevie for my mother.

Stevie touches everything and asks about a million questions at the same time. He also insists on singing one of his so-called entertainment songs as he whizzes up and down the aisles.

"Phone, phone on the range," Stevie sings. "Excuse me, Mr. Myers, what kind of instrument is this? Does it come in green? Green is my favorite color. What's yours? Can I try out these drums?"

"Settle down, Stevie," I say just like Pop tells him.

But Stevie doesn't listen to me.

When I told Denny about the guitar I was going to buy, he said, "You mean the red-and-black Stratocaster that's in the window?"

At the time I was helping him tape up a rock-and-roll poster of this jamming new band called The Edge. Denny's room had sheet music and CDs stacked in neat rows along the fringe of his rug. He was the rhythm guitar player in his band, Questions No Answers, which, by the way, practiced every Saturday afternoon in the basement of my house.

Denny stepped back and looked at his poster.

"I think that's the same guitar that Harry wants to buy," he said.

Harry Harrington, the *neighborhood-famous* lead guitar player in Denny's band? The one who was also in his first year of high school just like Denny?

"He can't buy it!" I said. "That's the guitar I've been saving up for."

Denny shrugged. He tightened the little rubber band on the ponytail he had just started to grow.

"Talk to Harry about it," he said. "Maybe you can work something out."

Talk to Harry? "No way," I told him.

And that's when I decided to go to Myers's Music first thing Saturday morning to buy it.

I stamped my sneakers on the school-yard ground as I thought about what happened next. No wonder I didn't have the time to write my sloppy copy. The whole weekend was one big family emergency. I had a perfectly solid reason for not getting around to writing it.

"How much longer do we have to be out standing in this *outstanding* school yard?" Robby Zao said, resting his chin on my shoulder. "There isn't even a fire."

Robby was right. There was no fire. Except for the one that was burning inside my brain. The bad news was that we would not be in this

outstanding school yard forever. Sooner or later we were going back inside, and I'd have to face Miss Fromme.

"All *outstanding* students return to class," Mr. Zifferman, the principal, said through his megaphone.

Miss Fromme raised her hand in a motion for her class to follow. The one thought that kept following me around was Stevie. Stevie who follows me into my room whenever I want to be alone. Stevie who tries to follow me on his Big Wheel whenever I take a bike ride. Stevie who wants to do everything that I do and then tells my mother all about it.

"Guess what, Flo?" Stevie says. "Brian took me to the music store again."

That really gets me boiling. Stevie chums up to my mother like there's no tomorrow. He even calls her Flo, which is short for Florence, and my mother allows it.

"After all, he *is* the baby of the family," my mother says.

"Baby my foot," I say. Stevie is nearly five years old and he's never even been to school.

One day Stevie asked Flo if he could stay at home with her instead of going to kindergarten.

And just like that, my mother said yes. I mean, nobody ever told me that I didn't have to go to school.

"Stevie will learn at home," my mother says. "He'll be all set by the time first grade rolls around."

Right. But who has to mind Stevie when my mother needs help? Me. And guess who'd rather be minding a bunch of monkeys on a desert island, lost forever somewhere in the middle of the Pacific Ocean, instead of watching Stevie? Me.

The more I thought about Stevie the angrier I got. Here I was, with my life in my hands, and it was all Stevie's fault. If it weren't for Stevie, I would have had my sloppy copy already written and ready to hand in to Miss Fromme just like everybody else.

Back in the classroom Miss Fromme had settled into her seat like a war pilot ready for takeoff. She hunched her back and held on to her desk. The kids at my table took one look at her and stood up without being asked. I shuffled my feet from side to side. I could already imagine the writing on my tombstone:

Brian Higman
Nice Kid
Better Luck
Next time

Maybe one day the fact would be that I would take over *The Franklin* and write my head off. But here were the facts today:

Number one: Miss Fromme was waiting for me to give her my written assignment.

Number two: I didn't have it.

Number three: I would not be seeing the light of day for the rest of the week if I didn't say something fast.

I stepped up to Miss Fromme's desk to give her
my blank piece of paper. Well,
it wasn't a completely blank
piece of paper. I had already
written my name on top. That
should count for something.

The closer I got, the braver
I became. I'd tell Miss Fromme
exactly what happened. At first
she would probably get a little
angry, but then she would probably understand. She'd proba-
bly give me a little extra homework. And I'd
probably do the same thing if I was her.

I smiled to myself. Everything would be fine.

So I did what any kid like me would do—I
ran for the bathroom pass. I slipped my paper

onto Miss Fromme's desk before it was even my turn.

I knew it was a dumb excuse to leave the room in such a hurry, but I needed more time to think. As I walked down the hall, I thought about Ana. Didn't I have enough problems already?

It never really bothered me that Ana was a girl. Our parents were friends, and we got along. I liked baseball. She liked baseball. I had a dog. She had a dog. We both liked rock and roll.

Then all of a sudden, things started to change. Ana didn't want to play baseball anymore. Me neither. We wanted to start a band instead. We bugged Denny to teach us how to play the guitar. Ana wanted to learn the bass. Robby Zao was taking drum lessons. Josh Mendez said he wanted to sing. Everything was going great.

But then Ana joined the orchestra. She took up the cello. Nadine Ali became her new best friend. Ana didn't come over on Saturdays anymore when Denny's band practiced.

"You can't just quit the band," I told her.

"What band?" said Ana. "You don't even have a guitar yet."

This was true. I didn't have a guitar yet. But all that was about to change. In the meantime maybe I will just put a personal ad in *The Franklin*:

Desperate:
 Soon-to-be great guitar player seeks bass player who feels the same.
 Must like rock and roll.
 SEND PHOTO!

On the way back from the bathroom, I could hear Miss Fromme reciting one of her favorite mottos: "Write about what you know. Or research what you don't."

I slinked into the classroom and put the bathroom pass back on the hook.

"Excuse me, Mr. Higman," Miss Fromme said. "You left me a piece of paper with your name written on it."

Miss Fromme folded her arms. She tapped her foot like she was in a hurry.

"Miss Fromme," I said. "I can explain."

"This is not the first time, Mr. Higman," she said.

Miss Fromme was right. It was the second time.

I knew that if I came home with another zero in English, I would be seeing a lot more than red on my mother's face. I think you'd call it fury. My mother didn't fool around with things like this. The last time she grounded me I had no TV or PlayStation for a week. This time could only be worse.

The newspaper headline would read:

BRIAN HIGMAN'S Mother
finally HITS CeiLING
Really nice kid banished to
SIBERIA for LIFE.

Miss Fromme lifted her reading glasses as if a cloud of smoke had just fogged her lenses. She stared at me with her red marker ready on top of my blank piece of paper. Well, not totally blank.

I was cooked . . . No! Baked. . . . No! Burnt to a crisp. I could see it in *The Franklin:*

Try This New Recipe!
Slow Roasted Surprise
Mix one big kid,
One late homework,
Add one angry teacher.
Turn on heat.
Stand back.
Expect anything!

"It was all my little brother's fault," I blurted out.

Miss Fromme narrowed her eyes.

Miss Fromme. Just the name gives me the same chill as fingernails on a blackboard. In my family her name comes with a reputation.

The only wish that Denny ever had for me was, "I hope you don't get 'The General.'"

"The General," as Miss Fromme was respectfully known throughout the entire Franklin Elementary School, was not a teacher to mess with.

"Don't let her fool you when she folds her hands and tilts her head," Denny warned me early on. "That mean's she's setting the trap."

Miss Fromme folded her hands and tilted her head.

"Go ahead, Brian," she said to me. "You have my full attention."

"Thank you, Miss Fromme," I said, nearly saluting her.

I raised my chin and began to tell her what had happened.

"It was Saturday. I was all set for the beginning of a great weekend. I planned to do my

homework after lunch, and I had the whole morning to myself.

"I looked over at the bed next to mine. Stevie was still asleep. He had all the sheets bunched up to his neck. Our dog, Patches, was snoring on a pillow next to him. Stevie and Patches—now that was a match! We were never allowed to have a dog in our house until the day that Patches arrived. And I do mean *arrived*, which by the way is another whole other story.

"One afternoon I was in the living room drawing these really cool planes with a new felt-tipped pen I got. My mother was nearby on her piano, trying to figure out a song she wanted to learn. It was raining outside like you wouldn't believe, when all of a sudden there was this sound.

" 'Hooooooooow.'

"It was the kind of sound you couldn't put your finger on.

" 'Stop your howling,' Pop said to Stevie. 'A man can't work with a noise like that.'

"Stevie looked out from under the kitchen table. He was counting the collection of banana stickers he had stuck underneath.

" 'That's not me, Pop,' Stevie said.

" 'Hoooooow wow!'

"The noise was beginning to bug me, too.

"My mother pushed aside her piano bench and wove a pencil through her hair.

" 'That noise must be coming from the washing machine,' she said. 'I think it's time for a new one.' My mother went to check the washer, but it was spinning fine.

"Meanwhile, I could hear my brother Denny in the basement singing through his microphone. It sounded more like an 'ooooooo' than a 'hoooow wow!' Shaver banged his crash cymbal and kick-drum pedal while the crystals on our chandelier shook each time Ace Randall hit a bass note. 'Twang, Twang, EEEEEEEEEE.' The neighborhood-famous Harry Harrington raised the volume on his electric guitar.

" 'Hoooow wow! Woooooooooo! Yoooow!' The noise was getting out of hand. I decided it was time to investigate."

I leaned against the white board and noticed that Miss Fromme was beginning to tilt her head the other way.

"And remember," I heard my brother's voice telling me. "If Miss Fromme tilts her head the other way, it means you need to use more descriptive language."

"**So I got up from my soft, comfortable green couch with the red-and-gold flowered pillows and decided it was time to investigate,**" I said it again only this time better. "**The annoying sound was coming from somewhere. It made the lamp shade shake like jelly.**" Hey! I thought. That simile was good.

Miss Fromme listened. She did not look impressed.

ALERT! RED ZERO CLOSING
IN ON ALL SIDES.
RUN FOR YOUR LIFE
IF YOU CAN!

Chapter Four
Fleas Not Lice

Position Wanted:
Experienced person needed
to help dig kid out of deep trouble.

That's how the classified ad in The Franklin *was going to read when I got around to writing it.*

"Sorry, Miss Fromme," I said, trying not to lose my train of thought. "I think I lost my train of thought."

Miss Fromme glared at Robby Zao who was laughing in his seat.

"Mr. Zao," Miss Fromme said firmly. "Is your writer's journal opened and ready? Or do you want extra homework?" Then The General turned to me. "Brian, please take your seat and see me after lunch."

"Miss Fromme?" Josh Mendez said in a whisper, as he barely raised his hand. "I'm supposed to go to the nurse's office and take my antibiotic now. I had strep throat all weekend."

Miss Fromme did not look happy. Thanks to my undone but soon-to-be, I'm sure, finished sloppy copy and a school fire drill, Miss Fromme's morning class time was quickly slipping away. She took the note from Josh's mother.

"Brian," Miss Fromme said. "Please accompany Josh to the nurse."

"But, Miss Fromme," I said. I held out my hands. I couldn't believe I was actually speaking. "I was just about to include some very important and descriptive information about the neighborhood-famous Harry Harrington."

Miss Fromme put both hands on her hips. "That won't be necessary, Brian," she said. "Class, let's get to our journals."

On the way to the nurse, Josh jiggled my sleeve. "You can tell me about Harry Harrington," he said. "I hate taking medicine. I need the distraction."

"Well," I said, "Harry Harrington is not

only neighborhood-famous because of his amazing guitar playing but also because of his two beautiful older sisters."

"I saw them once in a car," said Josh.

I nodded my head. "Harry told my mother that his parents paid more attention to his sisters than they ever did to him. He said it made him feel about as worthwhile as a flea."

"I had lice once," Josh said as he scratched his head.

"Fleas are different," I told him. "Fleas are something that my mother seems to have a soft touch for. She told Harry Harrington that he was more than welcome to 'come by the house anytime.' Harry took my mother at her word and started showing up for dinner nearly every single day. Once he even cooked us his recipe for chicken à la mode. Which, by the way, was not half bad."

"Chicken à la mode?" said Josh. He rubbed his belly. "I never heard of that before. But I wish I had some now."

We made a turn past the "Who's Who in School" bulletin board. Ana's face was plastered alongside the poem she wrote on leaves.

LEAVES
by Ana Newburg   Miss Fromme

Falling, falling from the trees,
Gold and red and orange leaves.
Children jump in raked-up piles,
Dogs come sniffing with a smile.
Squirrels take some for their nest.
I like autumn. It's the best.

"Anyway," I went on. I shrugged off the poem. "It was so annoying having Harry Harrington around my house all the time. When I wanted to use the video game, he was already playing it. If I called my mother to tell her I'd be late or something, Harry Harrington would answer the phone. 'Higman residence,' he'd say as if he actually lived there."

Josh shook his head. "A flea," he said. "They're hard to get rid of."

"Exactly." I nodded. I was glad he was listening. "But then bad news turned into good news. Denny lent me his old acoustic guitar when I told him I wanted to learn. And now he

33

and Harry both take the time to teach me chords. G, C, D, A."

I showed Josh the tips of my fingers. "I'm already getting calluses," I said. "That shows I'm really practicing."

Josh and I walked into the nurse's office. Mrs. Dunn checked Josh's name off a list, then opened the door of the small refrigerator she kept next to one of the sickbeds. I positioned myself for a little rest.

"Don't lie on that," Mrs. Dunn told me.

"I'm planning on getting sick later," I told her. "Maybe I should just stay now."

My mind was swirling with so much stuff. I began to wish that I had a piece of paper with me. I had this urge to write it all down. That's when I knew I was really not well.

Mrs. Dunn filled a teaspoon with gross pink stuff. "This is the part I hate," Josh said. "Quick, tell me the rest." But Josh swallowed his medicine so fast there wasn't even time for a joke. Okay, so maybe now Josh was feeling a little bit better, but as soon as we left the nurse's office to walk back down the hall, I began to feel sick all over.

Chapter Five
Raining Cats and Dogs

In my head, I wrote The Franklin horoscope tip:

Caution! Planets are crisscrossing. This is NOT your lucky day.

I squeaked my sneakers down the hall. "I'm really in trouble," I said to Josh.

"No kidding," he said. "Wait until you get home."

Josh wiped a pink smudge onto his sleeve. "But getting back to that howling noise. The one you were telling us about in class. . . ."

The howling noise?

"Oh, right," I said. "You mean the *hoow-wooooow* that was coming from somewhere?"

35

"Yep," said Josh.

Then just like that, the soggy, rainy, wet morning came back to me as if it were only yesterday. . . .

"I left my plane drawings on the floor and got up from the couch to investigate the howling noise. I was just about to check inside one of the hall closets, when Stevie made one of his so-called beeline dashes from under the table and yanked the front door open.

" 'It's a dog,' said Stevie, bending over and practically dragging it into the house.

" 'How did he get here?' I wondered out loud.

" 'It's raining cats and dogs outside,' Stevie said. 'That's how he got here.'

" 'Raining cats and dogs,' my mother repeated over and over as she dried the mutt with a bathroom towel.

" 'That sounds like a newspaper headline,' said Pop.

" 'Look at his spots,' I said. 'They look like black and brown patches.'

" 'That's his name,' said Stevie. 'Patches.'

" 'It can't be his name,' I said. 'It's not our dog.'

" 'I'll run an ad,' Pop said. 'LOST DOG FOUND. WHITE WITH BROWN AND BLACK SPOTS.'

" 'Patches,' said Stevie.

" 'Right,' said Pop. 'And if no one turns up, we'll say he's ours and call it a day. Now how about some lunch?'

"Anyway, after running the ad for a couple of weeks, no one showed up, and that's how Patches arrived."

"Ha! Ha!" Josh laughed as we opened the classroom door. "That was a funny story."

Miss Fromme turned to look at us. She sipped some water.

"Okay, boys, now take your seats. We're on page thirty-eight in our math books," she said.

Nadine Ali raised her hand. The tiny gold bells on her bracelet jingled.

"Miss Fromme," she said. "I was just wondering about one little part in Brian's story. Was the *hooooow-wow* howling coming from a ghost or the wind?"

"It was a dog," said Josh. "That's how they ended up taking their dog, Patches, in and keeping her."

I folded my arms. So did Miss Fromme.

I had a quick flashback. I remembered Denny staring hard into my face like a comrade preparing me for battle.

"And if The General folds her arms, it means she's ready for war," he said.

"It seems like you have a captive audience," Miss Fromme said to me. She closed her pencil on page 38 and looked at her watch for the millionth time. "You have two minutes to finish."

I stood up straight. I thought about my options. Go into battle, or go home with a zero.

"**Well,**" I began. I started to remember. "**It was Saturday. . . .**

"**I slowly inched out of my bedroom, leaving Stevie and Patches to whatever sweet dreams a boy and a dog could have. I didn't want to wake them up. I was on a mission and it was a secret.**

"**I was about to dig up the peanut butter jar that I had buried in the backyard near my pop's garage. The peanut butter jar had all** the money I needed in it to buy the guitar I wanted.

"I shoveled out the jar with one of my mother's gardening tools and brushed off the dirt. I held up the jar to look inside. Everything was still in there. I walked up the back porch steps and smelled coffee already brewing from the kitchen. Pop was up and reading the Saturday morning edition of the newspaper.

" 'Got plans?' he asked, looking over his paper. He dripped a teaspoon of honey onto his toast and paid close attention to the peanut butter jar I was holding in my hand.

" 'See this?' I said. I unscrewed the top and took out the sock that I had stuffed with money. Actually, there were two socks. One sock had the money. The other sock had more socks stuffed inside. That was my decoy. Just in case anybody ever found the jar and tried to steal it.

"Pop watched me pour about a pound of cornflakes into an ice-cream bowl. He looked at the crumbs of dirt that circled the jar around the table.

" 'Yep,' he said. 'I see it.'

"I held up the sock. 'I saved enough money in here to get myself an electric guitar. Denny said I could borrow his amplifier whenever he wasn't using it. I'm starting a band.'

"I could see right away that Pop was impressed.

" 'I admire a boy with gumption,' he said.

"Translation: a kid like me who could take it upon himself to have the courage to do something *outstanding*.

"All of a sudden I began to hear a stirring at the top of the stairs. The house was waking up. Steps padded closer to the landing. Milk dribbled down my chin. A flurry of paws clicked their way toward the back steps leading into the kitchen. It was Patches. That meant that Stevie was not far behind. I imagined my brother wide-awake and full of so-called entertainment.

" 'Peanut sat on a railroad track. . . . Toot! Toot! Peanut butter!'

"Oh no! Pretty soon my mother would be asking, 'Brian, honey, I need your help to keep an eye on Stevie while I give a piano lesson.'

"No way! I didn't want to take Stevie with me while I picked up my new guitar. This was going to be a moment in time that I wanted to remember forever! In a good way, I mean.

" 'Got to go, Pop,' I said in a rush.

" 'What's your hurry?' Pop asked me. 'How about some company?'

"I grabbed my sock and gave him a hug. Me and

Pop. Wow! What a morning! What could be better than that?"

Miss Fromme took a deep breath. "Two minutes are up," she said.

"Phew." I waved my hand like a fan in my face. "It's getting hot in here."

Ana tilted her head to one side and sat back like Miss Fromme.

"Can we hear the rest?" Robby asked, turning his seat toward the white board. "It sounds like something's going to happen."

"Something *is* going to happen," I told Miss Fromme. I slinked back to my chair. "It's not an excuse. It's a reason with gumption."

A reason with gumption, I thought to myself. I'll have to write that down in my journal. Maybe I should start a vocabulary section in *The Franklin*.

STEW: To cook by boiling slowly: To worry, as in to stew in one's own juices.

42

That was me. I was slowly boiling, and Miss Fromme looked like she was just about to raise the heat. She got up from her chair, pushed in her seat, and began to walk toward my desk.

Chapter Six
Fried to a Crisp

If I ever write an entertainment section for The Franklin, *I might not include a crossword puzzle. I do not like fitting words into boxes that meet across and down with a joining letter in between.*

I am more the word-jumble type. The word I am thinking of now is:

LEHP!

I watched Miss Fromme slowly making her way toward me. All of a sudden the loudspeaker crackled.

"Please excuse the *outstanding* interruption," Mrs. Confrontini, the school secretary, said. "Will the *outstanding* Brian Higman please report to the office."

Oh no. I wasn't even in trouble yet and I was already in trouble.

I looked at Ana. Even she looked nervous.

Miss Fromme leaned over to open the window. "Robby, please accompany Brian to the office," she said without even looking.

Out in the hallway Robby said, "Whoa! Are you just lucky, Big Hig? Or are you really in trouble?"

"I don't know," I said to Robby. "But I'm going to find out soon."

"Speaking of finding out," said Robby. "Are we starting the band or not? Did you get the guitar? What's going on?"

It was a good question. But it was not a question that I was ready to answer. I was still thinking about me and Pop on Saturday morning as we walked toward Myers's Music.

"It was just like one of those mornings you'd see in the movies," I told Robby, even though he didn't ask. **"The sun was out, the sky was blue, and the birds were singing a tune. . . .**

"I liked spending time with Pop alone. It was a rare occasion when Pop had a Saturday off from work. Being a salesperson was not an easy job. Especially on Saturdays. Pop said it was like the whole world was out buying refrigerators and ovens on Saturdays.

"We crossed the street and I hummed a little tune. Me and Pop on our way to the music store. That was something to sing about. But just as we turned onto Station Avenue, I looked down the block and saw someone familiar. It was Harry Harrington. Where was *he* going at this time of day? He was coming our way. He was heading toward Myers's Music. . . ."

There was a brown paper bag on Mrs. Confrontini's desk. It had my name written on it with crayon. It was my lunch.

"Hello, Brian," Mrs. Confrontini said. "It's

nice to see you again. Your mother dropped this by for you."

I tried to smile for Mrs. Confrontini.

"And by the way," she said, "I finally had the chance to meet that little brother of yours. The one that you were looking for the other day? I hear he'll be coming to school next year."

"Was he wearing two hats?" I asked.

Mrs. Confrontini laughed. "Yes, he was," she said.

I knew it. Stevie had stood in front of Mrs.

Confrontini's desk still wearing the raccoon cap with the earflaps snapped and the sailor hat on top.

"Since when does your brother wear two hats?" Robby asked me on our way back to class.

"Since two days ago," I said.

Miss Fromme glanced over and waved us in.

I crumpled my lunch bag inside my desk, opened my book, and got to work. Who cared about a zero anyway?

I'd start a "Manners" page for *The Franklin* and settle things once and for all.

Dear Manners Matter,

Do you think it is bad manners for a teacher to fail an unfortunate yet <u>outstanding</u> student without listening to his whole reason first?

Yours truly,
A Really Nice Kid

Dear A Really Nice Kid,

It would be very bad manners, indeed.

Sincerely,
Manners Matter

Kids all over the world would thank me.

I raised my hand. Miss Fromme shook her head. There would be no more interruptions for the rest of the morning.

We went through a lesson on identifying clouds. Cumulus clouds were puffy and piled up. Stratus clouds could be flat or layered or both. Cirrus clouds were curly.

We also had the pleasure of taking a pop math quiz on two- and three-digit division.

It was nearly lunchtime by the time Miss Fromme looked up and said, "Somehow, we have gotten through everything. Brian, I am still interested in hearing how your story ends."

What's this? I thought. The General is giving me another chance? The rest of my life could still be saved.

"You were telling us something about a guitar?" Miss Fromme said.

"You missed a lot," Robby Zao informed everyone. "Big Hig and his pop were just about to buy the guitar he saved up for when the neighborhood-famous Harry Harrington showed up at the same time."

Miss Fromme lifted her eyebrows and smiled like she was worried. "Go ahead, Brian," she said.

"Me, Pop, and Harry stopped right in front of the music store.

" 'What are you doing here?' I said to Harry.

"Harry smiled and shook hands with Pop. Harry's flannel shirt hung loose around his shoulders. I wanted a shirt like that.

" 'I was just on my way to your house,' said Harry.

" 'A likely story,' I said to myself.

"I reached into the pocket of my jeans and took out the blue-speckled Fender pick that Denny had given me. It was a medium.

Denny told me, 'A good guitar player is always ready to play.' That was me. And in about five minutes I'd have the guitar to go with it.

" 'Morning, George,' Mr. Myers said to my pop. 'Morning, fellows,' he said to us. Mr. Myers bobbed his head from side to side like a toy on the dashboard of a car.

" 'Where's that little brother of yours?' Mr. Myers asked me. He chuckled and gave Pop a wink.

"Pop stood smiling with his hands folded and his head shaking. He looked like he was praying for Stevie and understanding Mr. Myers at the same time.

" 'That little guy is really something,' Mr. Myers said, as he unlocked the front door. 'Just give me a minute inside.'

"We all waited while Mr. Myers got settled.

"I looked at Harry. He wasn't talking and neither was I.

"I cupped my hands around my face and pressed my nose against the window. There it was. The red-and-black Stratocaster. A glimmer of sun hit it just right, and it shined like a million bucks.

"Mr. Myers was taking his sweet ol' time.

He was turning on the lights, turning back the CLOSED sign to OPEN.

" 'Come on, come on,' I said to myself. I kept my sneaker close to the door, so I'd be the first one inside.

" 'Brian's here to buy a guitar,' Pop said all of a sudden to Harry.

"Harry shuffled a few pieces of gravel to one side.

" 'Want some help picking it out?' he asked me.

" 'No thanks,' I said just like that. 'I've got my guitar all picked out, and I have the money right here.'

"That's when I pulled out my sock. Only when I pulled out my sock, another sock fell out, and another and another.

"I had taken the decoy by mistake! My dreams were ruined.

" 'I have to go home,' I said to Pop. 'I'll be right back.'

"I took off running like an Olympic racer, darting around people and jumping curbs. 'See you,' said Harry as he gave me a wave. And when I turned the corner I saw him walk into Myers's Music."

The lunch bell rang and nobody moved. Well, nobody except me. I was starving after a morning like this.

"What a flea!" Josh mumbled.

"Brian," Miss Fromme said, "I have been very patient with you this morning. I think you will agree to that. But the fact of the matter remains. You do not have your written assignment. Please see me after lunch."

I could feel my eyes beginning to glaze.

"Does this mean I'm getting a zero?" I asked. I might as well know now before I tried to eat anything. The sloppy copy loomed in the distance like a threatening weather report.

WiLL the Hurricane Hit?
the Franklin reported.
Stay tuned for more
DISASTrous NEWS.

"After lunch, Mr. Higman," Miss Fromme said firmly. Then she pointed the way toward the cafeteria as if I might have forgotten.

→WANTED DEAD OR ALIVE ←
Brian Higman
Alias: BIG HIG
REWARD

"You're in deep trouble now," Ana said to me in the cafeteria as she walked past my table with her lunch tray and sat down right behind us. "You can't fool Miss Fromme with that story of yours."

"I don't mess with the facts," I said, reciting Pop's favorite motto.

Robby Zao ripped open his vegetarian wrap.

"She's right," Josh said. "Miss Fromme will never believe you."

I was about to take a bite of my ham and cheese when I noticed a pink piece of paper inside my sandwich. I pulled it out. It was a note from my mother.

Hi Honey ♡
Family meeting after School! Try not to be late. Stevie has a surprise. Love, xox Mom

I wiped the mustard off it and stuck it into my pocket.

"Why does your mother leave notes in your sandwich?" Josh asked me.

"My mother is not normal," I said.

Nadine Ali opened her chips. "I think your mother is fun," she said. "Remember the time we had a cookout in your backyard and it started to rain?"

Ana was listening. She pointed a carrot

stick toward our table. "I was at that cookout," she said.

"Ha! Ha!" Robby laughed. "We all got stuck eating soggy hot dogs and hamburgers inside your garage when the backyard drain clogged up."

"Remember?" said Josh. "And the backyard puddle got bigger and bigger until the tips of our sneakers were wet?"

I pictured the moment in my head. Me with my baked beans rolling off the side of my plate as we all pushed further inside the garage. We watched as my mother shuffled dinner plates onto this huge puddle like a deck of cards, while the rain cleaned the dishes for her.

"I think it was a good idea," said Nadine.

"I agree," said Ana.

In front of the cafeteria, Mrs. Wagner, the P.E. teacher, turned up the volume on Beethoven's Fifth Symphony. This was her signal for us to begin cleaning up our trays.

I, Big Hig, personally did not mind when Mrs. Wagner played her weekly tunes of classical music. Every week she had a new theme. All the composers had weird names. Last week it was Bach. The week before that it was Vivaldi.

Mrs. Wagner told us she got the idea from a circus trainer who tamed wild beasts.

"Okay, *outstanding* students," Mrs. Wagner said. "Let's get ready to go outside."

In the school yard, the kids from Miss Fromme's class were starting to crowd around me.

"Did you get the guitar?" asked Tyrone.

"What happened?" Chris C. wanted to know.

"I think Harry bought it," Jacelle said. Ana and Nadine and Martin Adaji moved closer to me like ants to a crumb.

I clawed my fingers through the chain-link fence. I was as angry as a wet hen just thinking about it.

"It was all downhill from there!"

"I left Pop at the music store, ran home, sprung the back door open, looked on the kitchen table, and saw that my sock was gone. The peanut butter jar was right where I had left it. So was the ice-cream bowl with half a pound of cereal still inside.

58

" 'Where's my money?' I shouted.

"I checked underneath the table to see if Stevie was playing 'bank.' He wasn't.

" 'Anybody home?' I yelled. No answer. Not even Patches came running.

" 'Looks like the troops have gone,' said Pop. The screen door closed behind him.

" 'Pop!' I said. 'My money is gone.'

"Pop rested his thumbs inside his pockets. I was glad he had followed me home. 'That money's got to be here somewhere,' he said.

"I rushed upstairs to check out Stevie's so-called hiding places, while Pop searched the whole downstairs. I looked inside the spaghetti pot that Stevie kept under a blanket. I crammed my way through his secret shoe pile. I scavenged through his hat collection. No luck.

" 'Any luck?' I called out to Pop.

" 'Not yet,' he said. 'Check with Denny.'

"I squeaked the door open to Denny's room.

" 'Denny! Denny!' I tapped his pillow. 'My money is gone. My sock is missing. It was on the kitchen table. Did you see it?'

"Denny rolled over and squinted his eyes.

" 'What time is it?' asked Denny.

" 'Great, just great,' I said to myself as I closed the door to Denny's room. Denny didn't know where my money was. He didn't even know it was nearly noon.

"I went downstairs and found Pop in the kitchen.

" 'It's not upstairs,' I said to Pop. 'I looked all over. It's gone.'

"Just then, Pop pitched his thumb toward a pink note on the refrigerator:

> Went to library.
> Stevie and Patches
> with me.
> Love,
> Mom xox

"Pop opened the kitchen cabinet and grabbed two granola bars.

" 'Come on,' he said. 'Let's go.'

Mrs. Wagner blew the school-yard whistle. "All *outstanding* boys and girls please line up for class," she bellowed through the megaphone.

"What happened next, Big Hig?" Josh asked.

"No talking, please," Mrs. Wagner said.

Josh shrugged his shoulders and lined up with the rest of the *outstanding* students of Franklin Elementary. At least my mother had packed me an *outstanding* lunch. I needed the strength. After all, I was just about to come face-to-face once again with the *outstanding* General Fromme.

NOW HEAR THIS!
REPORT TO BATTLE STATIONS!
THE SHIP IS GOING DOWN!

Chapter Eight
An Illuminating Mess

Outstanding Joke:

Question: Why did the centipede cross the road?
Answer: To get to the other side.

I was not in a funny or original mood.

When we settled back into the classroom, Josh Mendez asked an *outstanding* question.

"Miss Fromme, isn't Brian's story like a *verbal* sloppy copy?"

If I would have had braces, you would have been able to see them flashing a smile in the afternoon sun. Josh was right! I meant to give Miss Fromme a *verbal* sloppy copy all along! It was an experiment.

Miss Fromme thought about it for a moment.

"You could say that, Josh," Miss Fromme said.

Could this be true? Was Miss Fromme actually going to set me free and believe my bonafide story? A rush of relief swept over me. I was no longer a captive! Blue skies were on their way.

Suddenly Miss Fromme arched her eyebrows. You could even say that she looked kind of sorry for what she was about to say next.

"However," said Miss Fromme. "That was not the assignment. The assignment was a *written* sloppy copy, and in all fairness to everyone, Brian did not do that."

"But his money was stolen!" said Fareed.

"He was just about to go and get Stevie," Joelle hollered.

"Harry Harrington, that flea!" said Zachary.

"Excuse me," Miss Fromme said. "But would this entire class like to stay in for recess tomorrow? Brian, may I see you for a moment?"

I buried my head in my hands. I felt the comfort of what an ostrich must feel like when it hides its head in the sand.

There was a knock on the classroom door. I looked up. It was our principal, Mr. Zifferman.

"Good afternoon, Miss Fromme," Mr. Zifferman said. "Good afternoon, *outstanding* students."

He lifted his shoulders and squeezed his eyes like a baby who just got tickled.

"I would like to introduce you to our new student teacher, Mr. Minty. Mr. Minty comes to Franklin Elementary fresh from State University," Mr. Zifferman said.

"*. . . Freddy, the Freshman, the freshest kid in town . . .*"

Oh no! One of Stevie's so-called entertainment songs was stuck inside my brain.

"Do you mind if we stay and observe for a while?" Mr. Zifferman asked.

"Not at all," said Miss Fromme. "Brian Higman was just about to finish a story."

"Is that right, Brian?" asked Mr. Minty.

"I'm kind of at the end," I said, hoping to change the *outstanding* Mr. Minty's mind.

All of a sudden I understood the difference between my life and the life of an ostrich. An ostrich would never have to speak in front of a principal or a new student teacher. I sideswiped a look at Robby Zao. He was shaking his head up and down like a bird that was trying to talk.

"That's all right," Mr. Zifferman told me. "Just make believe we're not even here."

I raised my eyes. I had to do it.

"Well," I said without even blinking. "**I was just about to go to the library with my pop to see if my mother knew where my missing sock with the money was.**"

Miss Fromme cleared her throat.

"Go on," said Mr. Zifferman.

"**I had a sneaky suspicion that my little brother, Stevie, could be at the bottom of the missing money.**

"**When I got to the library, Patches was tied to the bench outside. He wagged his tail when he saw me coming.**

"**'Good boy, Patches,' I said. And I gave him a pat.**

"**Inside, Stevie had made himself perfectly comfortable on the floor of the young-readers' section. He was taking the leftover clothespins that Mrs. Saha, the librarian, hadn't used to hang up her decorations and was attaching them to his shirt.**

" 'Look! I'm a porcupine,' Stevie said, standing up when he saw me.

"The clothespins were sticking out in crazy directions.

" 'Stevie,' I said. 'I have something really important to ask you.'

"By now my face was covered in sweat. I was panting.

" 'What's wrong?' my mother asked. She brushed my hair back with her hand.

" 'Mom!' I said. 'Did you see my sock? I left it on the table. It had my money inside. I was going to buy my guitar this morning, but somebody took my money.'

" 'You're going to buy a guitar?' asked my mother.

" 'I saw the sock,' said Stevie.

"I turned around. 'I knew it!' I yelled.

"Stevie saw the look on my face. It was the same look that I had the time he took my favorite shirt and used it to dress up a snowman.

"That's when Stevie threw his sailor hat on the floor and made one of his so-called beeline dashes, crashing his way past Mrs. Saha and charging out the door.

" 'Better go after him,' Pop told me.

" 'And come right back,' said my mother."

I stopped talking. It felt like a good time to take a break.

"Thank you, Brian," Mr. Zifferman said. "Later on, you can stop by my office and tell me the rest."

Miss Fromme cheerfully showed them both to the door.

I let out a breath that could have blown any stratus, cirrus, or cumulus clouds straight across the sky.

Josh Mendez raised his hand.

"No more questions," Miss Fromme said.

"But Stevie ran away," I said. "I tried to catch him, but I'm not a fast runner."

I sat back down as soon as I said it. I had crossed the war line. General Fromme did not like calling out. Ana Newburg raised her hand.

"Miss Fromme," she said. "Brian's story gave me a connection."

A connection? I thought. Wasn't that another one of Miss Fromme's famous mottos for writing? Make the connections whenever you can.

"When Brian told us about his little brother, it reminded me of my little sister, Bella," said Ana. "Every time we bring Bella to the supermarket, she takes cans off the shelves and puts them in our wagon. I could write a story about that."

Wait a minute. Was Ana trying to help me? I gave her a smile just in case she was. And then I took another chance.

"My brother was lost," I said to Miss Fromme. My arms began to wave and spin like a carnival entertainer. "We couldn't find him anywhere."

Miss Fromme was not smiling.

Her face looked flushed. She smacked down her book.

The battlefield is getting smaller. Enemy tanks are moving in. We need more troops! Quick! To the foxhole!

"It's practically the end," I said without thinking. I was wishing I had a white flag to wave.

"It *is* the end," Miss Fromme said. Her patience was gone. Her limit had been tested. "You will not be taking up any more of my class time," she said. "See me after school, Mr. Higman."

The ruling was in. I, Big Hig, would not be seeing the light of day for a good solid week. But that didn't seem to bother Miss Fromme. She went right on with her lessons.

"Writers' journals open and ready," Miss Fromme said for the second time today. "Kayla, what did you write about yester-day? And how did you illumi-nate the moment?"

"I wrote about the expression on my grand-mother's face as my mother lit the candles on her birthday cake," she said.

"Very nice," Miss Fromme said. "How about you, Martin?"

Martin Adaji pointed his finger. "I saw a squirrel. His tail was fluffy and bent like a comma. That's all I wrote," said Martin.

"Good simile," said

Miss Fromme. "Boys and girls, you have twenty minutes to illuminate a moment. If you can't think of anything, look inside your journals for your seed ideas. Ready? Begin."

Miss Fromme set the timer and we all got to work.

I spiraled to a clean page and found my pencil. Before I wrote, I pictured the whole thing in my mind.

I left the library running after Stevie, following his trail of clothespins. "Hooooooow woooow," Patches was howling near the library bench.

"You can't leave that dog here," Mrs. Saha said. "He'll upset the whole neighborhood."

"Take Patches with you," my mother called after me. "And come right back with Stevie."

I looked for Stevie down the block.

"There he is," I shouted to Pop. "I'll get him."

It wasn't hard to see my brother. Stevie was the only kid running down the block wearing a raccoon hat with clothespins falling off him. He made a quick getaway into somebody's backyard.

Where was he going? I got to the driveway and stopped.

"Hello, Brian," Mrs. Confrontini said. "Are you enjoying your weekend so far?"

Mrs. Confrontini, the school secretary, was watering the flowers on her porch. I never even knew she lived there. "Hello," I said. Not sure what to say next.

Patches sniffed the edge of her lawn.

I scribbled down what happened next.

"Are you looking for something?" Mrs. Confrontini asked me.

Mrs. Confrontini did not have radar. My feet were stepping from side to side. My shirt was hanging out of my pants and one of my sneakers was untied.

"I'm looking for my little brother," I said. "You haven't met him yet."

This was before she had the pleasure of meeting Stevie today when he brought my lunch to school with my mother.

"What does he look like?" asked Mrs. Confrontini.

I shook my head at what I was about to say.

"He's about this big," I said, holding my hand up to here.

"Yes?" said Mrs. Confrontini.

"And he has on a raccoon hat with earflaps that snap underneath," I said.

"Yes," said Mrs. Confrontini.

"...And clothespins sticking out of his shirt."

Mrs. Confrontini tapped her watering can. "I did see a boy who looked like that," she said. "I think he went in there."

Riiiiiiiiiing! The buzzer went off on Miss Fromme's desk.

"Time's up," she said. She clicked off the timer.

And the rest of the day was a blank.

When the three o'clock bell rang, I was startled out of my social studies book. "Ponce de León," I said as Miss Fromme mentioned something about discovering Florida.

The class stood up and began to gather their books and backpacks and jackets from the hall closet. Some of them made sure they had copied down their homework assignment for tomorrow. Others, like me, simply slid their social studies books into their desks and waited to see Miss Fromme. Josh and Robby huddled around.

"We're still starting the band, right, Big Hig?" Robby asked me.

"It's just a matter of time," I said.

Miss Fromme began to erase the board.

"Good luck," said Josh. "Things can't get much worse."

I rubbed my head. "You wish," I said. It was the story of my life.

Chapter Nine
The Last Chance

EXTRA!
Brian Higman sets universal record for most detentions in world history.

When the classroom was empty, Miss Fromme made some space on her desk. She pushed aside some books and folders and papers and then waited for me to step forward.

"I'm really sorry, Miss Fromme," I said.

I kicked the leg on her desk by mistake.

"You had a busy weekend, Brian," Miss Fromme said. She almost sounded nice.

I tried to remember what Denny had told me to do if Miss Fromme ever sounded nice. I scoured my brain. He never said anything. I was on my own.

caution: ALL transmitters are about to BLOW. THIS IS NOT A TEST.

"Miss Fromme," I said. "I'm not trying to fool you. Everything I told you is true."

Miss Fromme opened her top desk drawer. She took out a box of crackers and placed three on a napkin for me.

"Here," she said. Then she pushed up her chair. "Why don't you tell me the rest."

"I looked for Stevie all over Mrs. Confrontini's yard. I looked behind the concrete birdbath and inside the garden shed. I looked under some bushes and got little green pieces of fern stuck in my hair. But I couldn't find him.

"Patches began to pull on his leash and bark in a different direction. He must have picked up Stevie's scent.

" 'Good boy, Patches,' I said, letting him take the lead.

"Patches led me three houses down from

Mrs. Confrontini's house right to where Harry Harrington lived. That's when I saw Stevie.

"He was sitting on the front steps with Harry's two beautiful older sisters. One beautiful sister was helping Stevie untangle a couple of twigs that got twisted in his T-shirt. The other beautiful sister was straightening out his raccoon hat. I had never exactly met Harry Harrington's two beautiful older sisters. And this did not seem like the best time to introduce myself.

" 'He's so cute,' the first beautiful sister said to me. 'Is he your brother?'

" 'We're thinking of keeping him,' the other beautiful sister said.

"I was just about to say, 'Take him,' when I realized they might want to trade in Harry for Stevie.

" 'He's mine,' I said, raising my voice.

"Stevie got up. He bent his knees and jumped off the porch.

" 'Geronimo!' Stevie yelled. 'You'll never catch me while I'm still alive!'

"What was my mother teaching him at home? I rushed a quick good-bye to the sisters and took off after my brother.

"I held on to Patches's leash as we chased Stevie home.

"Denny's band was already rehearsing. The bass kick on the drum thumped like a heartbeat from inside my house. I could hear my brother's voice singing deep and low. Harry Harrington wailed out two lead notes.

"I stopped dead. The band was rehearsing. Harry was back from Myers's Music. Did he buy my guitar? I had to see. I pushed the basement window open. I couldn't tell. I stretched my neck. I thought I saw it.

" 'Hooooow wooooow!' Patches pulled away from the leash and began to bark up the maple tree.

" 'Stevie,' I mumbled. I ran to the tree and shook my fist.

" 'Where is my money?' I yelled to him.

"My brother had climbed up the maple again. There he was curled up on a branch. Stevie threw some leaves on my head.

" 'I'm not coming down,' he told me.

Miss Fromme stopped me right at the good part. I waited for the final blow.

"First of all," Miss Fromme said. "I can tell

you right now that this will never happen again."

"Never, Miss Fromme," I said.

"And second of all," Miss Fromme went on. "I would like to tell you, Brian, that everything you told the class this morning *and* this afternoon is exactly the kind of story that you could be writing down on paper."

I knew it had been a long day for me, but that didn't make any sense.

"Brian," she said. And she patted her desk. "I want you to write down the rest of your story."

"You mean I'm getting a second chance?"

"Write like you're talking to me," said Miss Fromme. "Remember, this is your sloppy copy."

I took out a blank piece of paper. I wanted to get this off my chest. I also had to get home for the family meeting.

Brian Higman   Miss Fromme
I was frantically shaking my fist up a tree when Ace Randall, the bass player in Questions No Answers, asked, "What are you doing?"
Her long brown hair was dyed blue on one side. She flipped it back.

"Stevie's up there," I said.

My brother Denny had stepped outside the basement and stood around the tree with the rest of the band.

Denny looked up. Stevie threw more leaves.

"Is this about your sock?" Denny asked me, brushing leaves off his shirt.

"It doesn't matter anymore," I said. "Harry already bought the guitar."

Harry Harrington made a face.

"Dude," said Harry. "Your pop saved the day. No way was I going to get into a family argument and buy that Stratocaster. He said that guitar was already yours."

In one fat second I loved my pop more than anything else in the world.

I didn't feel so bad about Harry either.

When my parents came back from the library, Pop got Stevie out of the tree.

"That was a plumb dandy mess you got yourself into," Pop told Stevie as he edged him down a ladder.

Stevie ran into my mother's arms. "Flo!" he cried. "I was stuck."

In the kitchen my parents sat us all down at the table.

"One of you will be punished," Pop said. "Which one will it be?"

All I could think of was, Great, punish Stevie. If it wasn't for him none of this would've happened. I would've already had my guitar. I would've had my homework done. I wouldn't be in this stupid kitchen. It was all Stevie's fault.

Stevie was sitting on the kitchen chair. His feet didn't even touch the floor.

"Punish me," I said to Pop. "I was the one who was supposed to bring him back to the library. I'm sorry I lost my temper."

Pop squinted an eye at me and patted my back.

"That's right, Brian," Pop said. "Bringing back Stevie was your responsibility. And just for recognizing that fact, you will not be punished this time. Sometimes a person can learn his lesson by having the gumption to admit it."

"Wow, thanks," I said. And I hugged him tight. I even gave Stevie a little rub, though I washed my hands right after.

Mom held the peanut butter jar in her hand. "Let's get this straight once and for all," my mother said. I looked up at the ceiling my mother was about to hit.

"Stevie, did you take Brian's sock?" she asked.

My little brother was sniffling into a napkin.

"No," said Stevie. "I didn't."

"It just didn't disappear," said my mother.

Pop took out his wallet and gave me twenty dollars. "In the meantime," he said, "how about we take a walk back to Myers's Music and put down a deposit on that guitar before anybody else decides to buy it."

My pop was a genius.

"I'm finished, Miss Fromme." I handed Miss Fromme my sloppy copy. I looked in my notebook to double-check that I had written down all my homework assignments.

"Thank you, Brian," said Miss Fromme. "I'll look forward to reading it."

RAH! RAH! The Loser ties in OVERTIME!

"And, Brian," Miss Fromme called as I was nearly free out the door. "There will be no more chances."

Chapter Ten
The Outstanding and Exuberant Brian Higman

I walked home from school in a fog. The sloppy copy was done. That was a load off my mind. But I still had the weight of the missing money on my brain.

When I finally arrived home from school, I opened the door to find everyone waiting for me in the living room for the family meeting. My mother was sitting on her piano bench with Stevie and Patches nearby.

Stevie was wearing only one hat this afternoon. It was the sailor hat. He was also wearing a pair of blue mittens with one of my mother's aprons tied around his neck like a cape. Pop and Denny were sitting on the couch alongside Harry Harrington and Darleen and Cynthia, Harry's two beautiful sisters.

"What's going on?" I asked. I dumped my backpack on the rug.

Stevie held out his arms like a game-show host.

"Hooow! Wow!" Stevie said. He crawled on his hands and knees with his mittens. *"Ruff! Ruff!"* Stevie panted and sniffed around.

Patches wagged his tail.

"When does it end?" I asked my mother.

Stevie kept barking and acting like a dog. He shook his head. He licked at the air. He pretended to dig for a bone under the rug.

"Ta! Da!" said Stevie as he clapped his mittens and pulled out the missing sock!

"My sock!" I said. "I can't believe it." I pulled it away, and Patches jumped up. He tried to wrestle the sock from my hand.

"He's the robber!" Stevie yelled, pointing a mitten at Patches. Then Stevie took a so-called flying leap off two pillows and yanked the sock from his paws.

So that was it? The mystery was solved.

I took my seat at the family meeting and listened to the story from Stevie.

It seemed that today, while I was in class,

Stevie had gone into the backyard to look for worms. Spying on worms was one of Stevie's so-called science experiments. While he was carefully laying the slimy serpents back into the dirt, he noticed Patches sniffing around near Pop's garage. This was not unusual. Patches is a big sniffer. But then Patches began to dig something up.

Guess what it was! You guessed it. My sock. Patches had buried it and Stevie had caught him returning to the scene of the crime.

Well, I never would have suspected that a

dog could be a robber. I am not even sure if you can call a dog a robber. All I know is that Patches was the one who took it. Patches was the first one down the back kitchen steps the morning I left with Pop to buy my guitar. He must have smelled my sock. Liked it. Chewed it around. Then decided to keep it for himself.

What a dog!

The next morning I couldn't wait to get to school. I placed my peanut butter jar complete with money and sock on top of my desk where I knew it would be safe. Stevie would watch it for me.

I finished my cereal and put my bowl inside the dishwasher. I checked my backpack to make sure that I had all my homework.

My mother checked my forehead.

Stevie and Patches came shuffling down the stairs.

"Bye, Brian," Stevie said. I gave him a wave.

"See you later, Flo," I said to my mother as I whistled out the door.

Did I happen to mention that Ana Newburg was no longer my ex-best friend? I walked right up to her in the school yard this morning and said, "Ana, today I am going to buy my guitar.

"Fact number one," I said. "We think you'd make an outstanding bass player. Fact number two: We want to start a band with gumption. Fact number three: . . ."

Fact number three? The *gumption* threw me off.

"Big Hig doesn't mess with the facts," Robby told her.

"We're calling ourselves The Pitt," said Josh. "Since we'll be practicing in Big Hig's basement."

Ana rubbed the tips of her fingers. I'll bet she had calluses just like mine.

"Okay," said Ana. "I'll be in the band. But I'm not quitting the cello. And Nadine is still my friend."

Nadine Ali shook the charms on her bracelet. "Maybe I can play tambourine?" she asked.

My life was beginning to take a new turn.

I had an idea for a letter I would write to *The Franklin:*

Dear Franklin Newsletter,

   As a neighborhood reader, I would like to compliment you on your creative paper, The Franklin Newsletter, Someday, when I finally take over, and write my head off, I will tell you how it saved my life.
   It has been a pleasure doing business with you.

                              Yours truly,

                              Brian Higman

Mr. Zifferman was happy to see me. I was happy to see him.

   It was my turn to be the loudspeaker announcer. I told him the rest of my story and then took a seat next to Mrs. Confrontini. When the Pledge of Allegiance was over, Mr. Zifferman handed me a piece of paper.

   "All set?" he asked.

   "All set," I said.

   The loudspeaker crackled.

   "The word of the day is *exuberant*," I read,

making sure that I did not hold my mouth too close to the microphone. "E-x-u-b-e-r-a-n-t. It is an adjective that means enthusiastic or lively. Today there will be no *exuberant* fire drills," I said. "We will be having *exuberant* chicken nuggets and an *exuberant* recess outside with the *exuberant* Mrs. Wagner after lunch."

Mrs. Confrontini turned off the switch.

"By the way," she said. "I'm glad that everything worked out with you and your missing sock. That story you were telling Mr. Zifferman sounded quite *exuberant*."

I was just about to tell Mrs. Confrontini that it was *not* a story, but then I realized it really was.

"It's historical nonfiction," I said.

In the classroom Miss Fromme handed back the sloppy copies from yesterday—including mine. Of course, there were a mess of suggestions and corrections, but I, Big Hig, did not really mind. I planned on keeping my five senses ready and alert for action. Sight, sound, smell, taste, and touch. My pad and pencil were in my top pocket. A true writer is always prepared to write. That was my new motto.

Chapter Eleven
A Happy Ending

After school, on the way back from Myers's Music, I carried my red-and-black Stratocaster in the new guitar case that Denny and Harry were able to get me for a bargain price. Even my pop had left work early to be a part of the *outstanding, exuberant,* and monumental occasion.

I guess you could say it was a family event.

My mother and Patches had showed up, too. Along with Darleen and Cynthia who held Stevie's hands while we were in the store.

"*Twinkle, twinkle, little guitar,*" Stevie sang.

"It's a beauty," Mr. Myers said. He counted out my money and tucked it into the register.

When I got home I played my guitar until it was time for supper. My mother whipped up my personal favorite—spaghetti and meat-balls.

"This is delicious," said Darleen.

"Mrs. Higman, may I have the recipe?" Cynthia asked.

Harry Harrington's two beautiful older sisters also said they'd be happy to stop by tomorrow to keep an eye on Stevie, if that was okay with my mother.

"Yes," I said. "That would be great. You're welcome to come by the house anytime."

As you can imagine, everybody went crazy when they heard about my guitar.

"You did it, Big Hig," said Robby Zao. "We're starting a band."

"Nice work, Hig," said Josh. He grabbed my hand and shook it.

The brand new day seemed destined to be bright.

Ana was the first one to put her homework into the homework bin on Miss Fromme's desk. Robby came back with Josh after accompanying him to the nurse. And Miss Fromme was standing in front of the white board, ready to set her timer.

"Okay, class," Miss Fromme said. "Fifteen minutes to write about a topic. Remember to visualize before you write and use your senses. Look through your journals for seed ideas if you need inspiration."

I flipped through my writer's notebook to see if I had any ideas.

Fishing trip with family . . . another zero . . . tomatoes are not only vegetables . . . a boy with gumption . . .

"Writers ready?"

"Miss Fromme," I said. I raised my hand.

I was just about to ask her if I could share a very descriptive and illuminated story about how our band, The Pitt, was going to enter the Franklin Elementary School Talent Show this spring.

But then I decided not to. Instead, I took out my sharpened pencil, smoothed open a clean page of paper, and wrote:

Brian Higman   Miss Fromme

    It all started yesterday when my
little brother, Stevie, had a
so-called idea....

Chapter Twelve
Big Hig's "FACTS" for Writing

➤ Big Hig's "FACTS" for Writing ←

1. Pay attention to the ordinary things that happen in your life and teach yourself to write them down.

2. Write about what you know OR research what you don't.

3. Organize your story with a beginning, a middle, and an end.

4. Think of the setting and the characters

5. Visualize the scene in your head.

6. Choose outstanding and descriptive word

7. Illuminate the moment including the five senses.

8. Don't be afraid to write with your voice.

9. Take a break if you get stuck.

10. DON'T GIVE UP !!!

BIG HIG'S DISASTROUS NEWSLETTER

as keyboarded on my computer by Brian Higman

WRITER'S JOURNAL UPDATE

Dear Writer's Journal,
   Today I do not have my homework and I am about to get another zero.
        Yours truly,
        Guess who?

← my mother

A PERSON WHO CAN MAKE A BIG DEAL OUT OF ANYTHING

Ana is the kind of person who can make a big deal out of anything. Last week when Martin Adaji put a tomato in his fruit painting, Ana made one of her big deals about whether a tomato was a fruit or a vegetable. I was glad when Mrs. Chila said that a tomato could be considered as both. It was a fruit that was used as a vegetable. In the plant group it was actually considered to be a berry.

← TOMATO

BRIAN HIGMAN'S MOTHER FINALLY HITS CEILING!

Really nice kid banished to Siberia for LIFE.
See more inside.

AHHHH

CAUTION:
Planets are crisscrossing.
This is **NOT**
your lucky day.

TRY THIS NEW RECIPE!

SLOW-ROASTED SURPRISE

Mix one big kid,
one late homework.
Add one angry teacher.
Turn on heat.
Stand back.
Expect anything!

artwork done by the outstanding Big Hig